THE WITCH'S OATH

Tiffany Ann

Publisher Tiffany Ann
www.tiffanyannbooks.com
ISBN: 9798394825026

Table of Contents

Dedication

This one is for the Colby who inspired the main character. And for Remy, who makes shift change so much fun.

Special Thanks

To my husband, my soulmate, my prince, thank you for your unwavering support, and for at least reading the smut scenes.

To R.C. Matthews for my cover.

To Connie B. Dowell, my editor and blurb writer.

To my faithful beta readers.

And to my first official ARC team.

Finally, to all the fans who are coming back for more. I couldn't succeed without your support.

Introduction

Welcome to my new series, *The Wardwell Witches.* This is a spin-off series from *The Soulmate Call Series.* It matters not if you have read the first series. However, if you haven't read it, I do hope you go back and fall in love with the Turners.

This series is primarily a romance series, yet it does contain good vs. evil. Therefore, there are darker moments and sinister antagonists.

I only have two planned in this series so far, but my hope is that more emerge as I get lost in these characters.

Correction, a third romance jumped at me the closer I got to the end of this story. This series will now be a trilogy for sure.

Will the Wardwells run into any of the Turners? I honestly don't know. Kenzie and Colby definitely will not.

*This story touches on many issues that may cause triggers. Alcoholism, suicide, drugs, and pedophilia. Please be advised if any of these are triggers for you.

*Note: The songs incorporated into this love story happen during pivotal moments. Moments where I wish copyright laws didn't prohibit me from copying and pasting the entire song lyrics as long as I gave credit to the songwriter. If it so moves you, I recommend pausing and pulling up the songs mentioned in their entirety during these moments.

Playlist

- "I Get to Love You" by Ruelle
- "When a Man Loves a Woman by Michael Bolton
- "Make You Feel My Love" by Adele
- "I Feel Good" by James Brown
- "A Thousand Years" by Fearless Soul
- "I Need You" by Tim McGraw and Faith Hill
- "I Got You Babe" by Sonny and Cher
- "Marry Me" by Train
- "How Long Will I Love You" by Ellie Goulding

Prologue

Revenge

Before you embark on a journey of revenge,
dig two graves. ~ Confucius

They call me Revenge. It's not the name my mother gave me, but it's the only name that suits me. Their pain haunts me day and night. Their cries call out to me wherever I go. I'm left with no choice but to answer.

"Tell me, dear one, who causes you to seek my services?" I asked the woman embarking on adulthood. The woman whose pain drew me to this city.

I feel no sympathy for her or her tormentor. I'm not here to ease her pain. I'm here only for what I gain from her desperation.

"I want to—forget. To move on, but every time I close my eyes I see his face. I smell his breath. I feel his body hovering above me."

"Who is this man you speak of?" I can almost taste the offering she will give me to satiate her need for revenge. I too must sacrifice a part of myself to complete the ritual. My sacrifices are worth it—they keep me beautiful.

My patience grows thin as the wretched soul struggles to name the one who brought us to this moment. I turn to leave—a bluff—one that always works.

"My uncle." She says to my back.

I wipe away the smirk of triumph that formed on my face before I turn back to face her.

"You understand there's a price to pay? What I do can't be done for free."

She nods her head.

I pull the rolled-up contract from my purse. It's just a formality. Whether they sign or not makes no difference. Verbal consent is all I need. I prefer the drama of watching them unknowingly sign their life away.

I slowly unroll the contract, for dramatic effect, mind you. I hold it open in front of her without bothering to set it on a hard surface. It makes for an awkward moment to stand in front of me to read the entire contract. If one put their pain aside for just a moment and took the time to read every word—they'd run the other way.

She's just like all the rest. Signs on the dotted line with no consideration for what she just signed.

My happy dance will have to wait. I wouldn't want her to question why her pain brings me so much joy.

I quickly roll up the contract before she can

change her mind.

"Last chance to change your mind."

Quickly, she shakes her head side to side. "No, it's the only way for me to find peace."

"Do you want to watch?" They always want to watch.

After a nod of her head, "Take me to him," I order.

We take my car across town. She'll have no need of hers once I'm finished.

She drags her feet behind me as we approach his front door. A quick knock and he answers. I hate it when I have to wait around for them to come home.

With one look at me and another behind to his niece, I give him that brief moment to take his last breaths. "*Iustitia*"

I never know how justice is going to play out for the ones I'm commissioned to exact revenge upon. Water bubbles up from inside of him. It leaks from his mouth as he chokes. His hands grip his throat in a futile attempt to grasp for air. Coughing, regurgitation, the works, as he drowns in front of us.

His niece doesn't scream or beg me to stop. They never do. I only hear the cries of those most genuine in their need for revenge. The wishy washy have no need for my services.

She's so busy enjoying her uncle's demise that she doesn't notice the sacrifice she's made leaving her body.

I feel it. I notice it. Her beauty washes over me like rain on a summer's day. I close my eyes and let it cover me from head to toe.

My work is done. I leave her to her short-lived victory. She won't even notice I've departed at first. She'll dance around with joy. Spin around as the feeling of freedom envelopes her. Might even go for a walk as she marvels that justice has been served.

She'll eventually catch a glimpse of herself in a mirror. In the end, the police will investigate her uncle's death. When she turns up as a suspect in the murder of her uncle, they will find her body somewhere. It'll be ruled a murder-suicide. It always is.

Revenge is sweet at first, but like the saying goes, "It's the aftertaste that's bitter." A taste so bitter that none can live with the sacrifice they made to get what they believed would fix all of their pain.

The new pain they bring upon themselves is a pain none can live with.

I, on the other hand, never lose any sleep over their need for revenge. I sleep like a baby, knowing I'll always be seen as beautiful.

"When you find the one who completes you, your soul will call their soul. You will become one in your hearts and minds. You will not be limited to communicate as humans are limited. As one heart, one soul, and one mind—your thoughts will be their thoughts and their thoughts will be yours."

"A spell that spans generations required much. I'd give anything to find my way to you again."

"Only if and when a Turner makes the right choice will a Wardwell birth another son and find a happily ever after with their soulmate."

~ Mercy Wardwell, 1693

Chapter 1

Kenzie

"Can I get a beer, beautiful?" the first customer of the night asked Kenzie.

"If that's a pickup line, it's terrible." She hadn't bothered to look at the man calling her beautiful while finishing cleaning the counter full of fingerprints left over from the night before.

"Angel, I just want a beer."

"I'm definitely no angel." She reached under the counter for a mug.

"Look, doll, I just want a beer."

With the newest demeaning name spewing from his lips, she raised her head to get a look at the offender. Daggers shot from her eyes, while she sucked in a breath at the sight before her. The finest specimen to ever catch her eye stood in front of her with an ego that needed proper deflating. "Do I look like a toy to you?"

"Sweetheart, who peed in your cheerios this morning?" Kenzie quickly averted her eyes from the deep, dark eyes staring back at her.

She pulled the lever to fill his cup with her

favorite brand on tap. "Do you still want this beer or not?" She set it down harder than intended. Foam drizzled down the side onto her clean bar top.

"Darlin', why wouldn't I want the beer I've been trying to get for the last couple of minutes?" He put the mug to his lips and drank the whole thing in one go, leaving foam across his upper lip. A deliciously thick lip she'd never enjoy anywhere on her body. Where did those thoughts come from? Thoughts she never allowed herself to entertain.

"Are you unable to talk to me without giving me a nickname?" *Yep, I'd much prefer deflection. I'm keeping my walls up and my attitude strong. Just because this stranger makes me thankful for my eyes, it doesn't change the way he grates against every nerve ending in my body.*

"What else should I call you? You're not wearing a name tag, gorgeous." This time, he winked while giving her yet another nickname.

"Can I get another?" he pushed the mug back toward her for a refill.

Kenzie pulled a Bud Light from the cooler beneath her. Popped the cap and slid it to him.

"Light beer, baby, seriously?"

"Well, *old man*, if you're not careful, you'll end up with a dad bod." The obvious age gap between him and her made no difference to her. She appreciated beauty in all ages and packages. If only she hadn't sacrificed the one thing she needed to benefit from a man she could clearly have beneath her before the night ended without even trying.

He placed his hand over his heart like she'd stung him. "Old man. Now who's tossing around nicknames?"

"What? You're not wearing a name tag either."

"Touché." He lifted the bottle in her direction before getting up from the stool and heading toward a table in the back of the bar with a group she hadn't noticed watching the scene unfold.

Her best friend, Remy, bumped her hip with his. "What did I just witness?"

"Nothing." She spat through gritted teeth. Saved by the group of girls who walked in the front door and headed straight for the bar to order drinks.

Chapter 2

Colby

Old Man, huh? Sure, he was pushing forty, but he didn't consider that made him old. Not yet. And sure, the sexy vixen bartender hadn't turned thirty. He guessed her to be in her mid to late twenties.

He didn't usually give women under thirty more than a passing glance. Which is all he intended to do when he went for a beer. Only she managed to crawl under his skin despite the chip on her shoulder.

Sitting with the guys didn't distract him from her beauty. He sipped his light beer while watching her pull her mass of chocolate waves into a messy bun before making the drink order for the group of women standing in front of her.

In a few days, he'd move onto the next city with his work crew and could put this woman out of his mind. She clearly believed him a player—like most women assumed. He couldn't figure out what gave ladies the impression he didn't want a committed relationship.

He couldn't ask the men he lived and worked with. They all looked at him as a hero. They hadn't figured out how much of what he told them was just talk. He picked up a few women on occasion, but not as many as he claimed.

Colby didn't seek out a reputation, like Sam Malone or Barney Stinson. It happened by accident.

Being on the road for work and living in hotels, not much of his life stayed private. His first night out when he took the job, he got lucky. He hadn't intended for his roommate or any of his coworkers to catch him coming out of her hotel room. His dick led the way the night before, keeping him from noticing the woman's room faced the breakfast area in the hotel lobby.

They all saw him sneak out of her room with his boots in hand. In typical male fashion, they hooted and hollered, causing a scene.

That being their first impression of him, they called him "player" from then on. His male ego liked the affirmation, so he let them believe what they wanted to believe. He allowed his pride to turn him into a liar.

His made-up conquests became the topic of conversation whenever they all had a few too many. The real Colby would never dishonor a woman by revealing anything that happened behind closed doors. His handful of hookups remained between him and her. Most of what he confessed to his friends never occurred.

He could probably write erotic fiction with all the stories he told in order to remain their hero with women.

The sound of piano keys shook him from the rabbit hole his mind wandered into.

"One look at you
My whole life falls in line
I prayed for you
Before I called you mine…"

That voice. The feeling behind the words to a song he'd never heard. He felt every word etching itself into his heart and mind.

His feet carried him toward the voice, pulling him. His sexy vixen sat behind the piano with eyes closed. She played and sang words more beautiful than anything he'd ever heard.

"Whatever may come your heart I will choose…"

"She's spellbinding, isn't she?" One of the girls at the bar from earlier tried to interrupt the moment capturing his heart. He ignored her.

"I get to love you…"

Colby wiped a tear from his eye. He hadn't cried since childhood. Where did that come from?

She looked up from the piano. Their eyes met. She gave him a half smile.

He'd only had two beers, yet it suddenly felt like he'd had twelve. The walls closed in around him. He struggled to pull air into his lungs. His eyes scanned for the nearest exit before making a dash into the fresh air.

Air that didn't last before the clouds opened, releasing a downpour. Colby looked up at the sky and let the rain wash over him until soaked to the bone.

It didn't help. It was as if his heart had never beaten before her voice slithered into his being. The feeling foreign and uncomfortable.

He had only one choice. Never return to this bar. Not even to this city if he could help it.

Chapter 3

Kenzie

Kenzie stroked the keys as the song ended. She only took the stage when a customer put in a request. A paid request. Usually, a lover brought in a date and offered the fifty dollars she charged to sing.

It mattered not if she'd ever heard the song. She only had to listen to the melody and the words one time before it flooded her heart and soul.

Just one performance drained everything from within her spirit.

Remy stood by with a glass of water and a cool cloth. "I swear, you release pheromones into the air when you sit behind that piano and open your mouth."

Kenzie sucked the water from the bottle until it crinkled with emptiness. "That's nonsense."

"No more nonsense than your lucky brew you sell in the back room."

Her body ached to lay down for the rest of the night, but she knew that option didn't belong to her. Not with the staff shortages everyone suffered. If she sat for a few more minutes, maybe her limbs would stop shaking.

"For someone who doesn't believe in love or want love, you reek of it when you sing."

When the lyrics and the music floated from her phone into her ear canal, something consumed her. An unexplainable overtaking. The feelings, the emotions that went into the writing of the song, became her feelings and emotions.

"These feelings are fleeting. They pass once the last words leave my lips."

"You keep telling yourself that."

"Why are you so determined to see me fall in love when you know I can't?"

"Curse, shmurse. Curses are meant to be broken. I've watched *Once Upon A Time.* All you need is true love's kiss."

"You know that's not how the curse will be broken." Kenzie tried to stand. She gripped the side of the piano to steady her shaky legs.

"Girl, take my arm. I'll help you to your room."

"It's too much work for you to do alone."

"Tracy is still here and kicking butt behind the bar. She'll help me close up."

Kenzie accepted Remy's arm. He escorted her through the back and up the stairs to her apartment. Why had this particular song on this night taken more out of her than all the others?

Remy maneuvered the self-made landmine

across her living room floor. Empty pizza boxes, clothes, shoes, and more were tossed about. She never entertained, so why bother with cleaning up when there was so much else needing her attention?

Remy slipped her shoes off and tucked her in tight. "One day, you're going to find that man that makes your toes curl, and he's going to run the other way because of this shit show you live in."

"You're hopeless, Remy."

"Girl, how can *I* be hopeless? I'm just confident you deserve good things, and they're coming. Despite everything you've given up."

Kenzie pulled the duvet over her head. It was pointless to argue with him. He knew her story, but refused to accept that in order to shrink his stage four cancer down to stage one—making it treatable instead of fatal—she gave up her arousal abilities.

They weren't coming back, and it was worth it. Worth having the one person in the world she could count on still with her—alive.

Her sister Leigh ran away at fourteen. Blocked their telepathic connection and never looked back. Kenzie didn't blame Leigh for running. Hell, she should have run with her. Maybe that was why Leigh cut her out of her life.

Kenzie tried to connect with her sister once their drunk piece of shit mother went to prison for manslaughter. In typical selfish fashion, their mom once again got behind the wheel of her car inebriated, only to kill a whole family driving home from a weekend getaway. Hopefully, dear old mom got the help she never would admit to needing once those prison doors slid shut.

Kenzie told Leigh about it through their link, but her sister never responded. Not once. Leaving her to only guess what Leigh could have done. She hadn't heard of anyone ever sacrificing the link between sisters for a spell, but maybe her sister did.

She rolled over while listening to Remy stumble around the living room. She'd wake up to find everything put away—she'd bet money on it. Remy couldn't stand clutter.

Chapter 4

Colby

It had been a few weeks since the seductive bartender had captured his eyes. More than his eyes. He couldn't stop thinking about her. So much so, he'd found the song she sang and played it on repeat. Like a lovesick sap. Knowing full well the chances of ever seeing her again were slim to none.

Mid-State Steel workers went from town to town, city to city, did the job and moved on. Sometimes those jobs lasted for months at a time, and other times they lasted a few days.

His company blew through her town in a whirlwind. Each new city, his crew found a local bar to unwind in at the end of the day.

Some were better than others. The one his co-worker Richard found for them in their current city only brought to mind the one he left behind.

It looked nothing like hers, yet it made him close his eyes to picture the haunted vibe of *The Witch's Brew.* From the broomstick logo on the uniforms, to the Halloween decorations everywhere he turned.

Colby sipped on his eighth beer of the night when a pretty little piece of ass sat down in the booth beside him. "Buy me a drink?"

Why not? Maybe she'd help him forget the woman he'd never see again.

He nodded.

She stood back up so he could maneuver out of the booth away from his friends acting like drunk idiots.

He stood at the bar and shouted to the bartender over the loud music. "Another beer, and whatever she's having."

She sipped on her vodka cranberry and gave him what he liked to refer to as bedroom eyes over the lip of her glass.

He needed a good fuck. Surely, emptying his ball sacks would help him move on.

Before the brazen redhead in the halter top summer dress got too drunk for his conscience, he asked her, "Want to go someplace quieter?"

"My place is only a couple blocks around the corner."

"Do you pick up men often and take them home?"

"Only when I have an itch I need scratched."

Colby's dick accepted the invitation as it pressed painfully against his zipper.

He stood up, hoping for discretion. The awkward movement hadn't gone unnoticed by the woman. Her eyes glanced down toward his crotch. She looked back up at him with her bedroom eyes again.

"Like what you see?"

"Let's go."

She hadn't offered her name, and he didn't ask. Why would she? She needed relief just as much as he did and had her own reasons that were none of his business.

She chatted incessantly on the five-minute walk to her apartment. Colby pretended to listen. His beautiful bartender kept popping up in his thoughts. Was she working tonight? What was she wearing? Was she seeing anyone? When was the last time someone made her scream out his name?

His hookup unlocked the front door of her place before turning and giving him those damn bedroom eyes that kept making his dick twitch.

Colby moved in to kiss her. She turned her head. "I just need a good fuck. We aren't in a relationship."

Whatever. No kissing. Fine by him. He'd never been a big fan of swapping spit, anyway.

Once the door shut behind him, she slipped out of her little dress. Nipples pebbled just for him. Brazilian bikini wax begging for him to dive right in.

She tossed a condom at him.

No foreplay seemed the way she wanted this experience to go.

Colby stripped out of his clothes and rolled the condom over his dick.

His date lay down on the couch. His fingers

moved her sweet lips to ensure he wouldn't hurt her.

"I'm ready, seriously. Just put it in and fuck me."

How did he keep ending up in these situations? He no longer cared about her needs and wants as he slammed into her. The slap of skin drowned out the voices in his head telling him to put his clothes back on and go back to his friends.

What did she need him for? Her fingers rubbed her clit until her pussy squeezed his appendage. She lay there looking at him with eyes that said, "Finish already."

Colby closed his eyes, trying to cum. That only made things worse as his bartender flashed before him. He couldn't take it anymore. He pulled out. Tossed the empty condom in the nearby trashcan. Put his clothes back on and headed out the door.

What the hell? That had never happened to him before.

He walked right back to his friends. He needed more beer.

They congratulated him. Assuming he got what he left for and had come back to celebrate. He needed a hole to bury his head in. Instead he drowned his woes with a bottle of Coors.

Chapter 5

Kenzie

Kenzie descended the stairs from her apartment with dread. Lacking the energy to move down them with one foot behind her, she stepped down and dragged her other foot to join her before taking the next step.

Her mother had opened the bar when Kenzie and her sister were still toddlers. She couldn't remember a time before her days and nights were spent at *The Witch's Brew.*

If her mom had set up the room above the bar and made a home for them, maybe she wouldn't have killed that family.

Or she'd have killed someone else on her way to buy milk or something.

A full-blown alcoholic and a bar made for a dangerous combination.

It all started innocently enough. Her mom opened the bar and sold a special potion to an elite clientele who sought her services. Just a drop, no more, and the recipient lived the rest of their life surrounded by good luck.

Her mom never shared what it cost her to set up her brew. She'd only made the one batch, which never ran out.

Kenzie inherited the brew after her mom's incarceration. Clients preferred purchasing a drop in the early morning hours. A morning person she was not.

Brring, brring. Her newest anxious customer repeatedly pushed the button for entry before she made it to the last step.

"Mr. Steele, I presume?" Kenzie opened the door to a young man fresh out of college. He came dressed to impress in his navy, three-piece suit.

All her clients were either Mr. or Mrs. Steele. Kenzie's grandmother had been a fan of *Remington Steele,* and in honor of the woman they all missed dearly, her mom chose Steele for ambiguity purposes. Their clients valued their privacy.

It couldn't get out that a Senator or a well-known businessman had come to a witch for a potion.

Mr. Steele stepped through the doorway, looking around nervously.

"Let me get some coffee, and I'll be right with you." She never could go back to sleep after waking up for the day, so she needed lots of caffeine to keep from biting anyone's head off.

She dragged herself to the back room where she kept her Keurig and grabbed the peppermint mocha creamer from the fridge to pour into the empty cup, a trick she'd learned at a friend's house years ago. Pour the ice-cold creamer in first, and it doesn't cool down the coffee.

Kenzie grabbed the hot addiction to soak up the aroma before taking her first sip. *Ah,* just what the morning called for.

She found Mr. Steele pacing the floor of her bar. His parents and maybe even grandparents were clients—most certainly. Only way someone so young might have known to seek her services. She wouldn't ask, and he wouldn't tell. Confidentiality.

Mr. Steele pulled out an envelope with ten thousand dollars in cash stuffed inside. Kenzie imagined him a man on his way to law school or some other prestigious field.

She pulled the bottle from her pocket. "Stick out your tongue." She opened the container and carefully put just a drop in the dropper. No need to waste any of it. Her client obeyed without question. *"Fortuna."* She spoke the word for luck in Latin. An unnecessary part of the process, but one that clients expected. For whatever reason, they took offense when the witch they paid didn't cast-a-spell.

Mr. Steele nodded his thanks and left without a word.

Over the years, her mom recognized individuals who'd paid her a visit, and so had Kenzie. They'd show up in the news or on social media. Luck indeed followed them after they left *The Witch's Brew.*

Chapter 6

Colby

The universe had a funny sense of humor—not. Sevierville, Tennessee. The only place in the whole damn world he never wanted or expected to find himself in again. His company finished the last job under budget and under schedule. A onetime in and out job. Come to find out, it had been more like a job interview.

For the next year—at minimum—his crew would live and work in the only place that haunted him. The place where his bartender lived.

The company in Tennessee set them up with a couple of Airbnbs a mile from *The Witch's Brew.*

His crew had come home from their first day of work, anxious to hit the bar to celebrate the guarantee of a steady paycheck.

The knots forming in his gut tempted him to crawl into the twin size bed in the room he shared with his roommate. The pull to see her again, against his better judgment, yanked his feet toward her.

Despite the warning bells ringing in his head—like that he was in Tennessee only temporarily, the age difference, the chilly vibes she put off when he spoke to her…the list could go on—he still showered, combed his beard, slipped on a baseball cap to hide his bald head, and splashed one of the colognes from his collection on his neck.

They hadn't had a chance to stop for groceries, so he'd grab dinner at the bar, too. If his stomach would even hold down a meal.

His slippery hands slid off the door handle he tossed open. Damn sweaty palms—he hadn't experienced clammy hands since he was a teenager. Could she have cast a spell over him? Ha. If he believed in witches, it would explain everything.

Colby froze, mesmerized at seeing her again. A small part of him feared she'd moved on to another job, the turnover in the workplace being so high in this economy.

Chestnut waves gathered haphazardly into a bun. Flyaway strands outlined the face of an angel. Stormy eyes filled with laughter over something the male bartender said to her. The giant African American man wearing a t-shirt that said, *Don't Kill My Vibe,* would have sparked the green-eyed monster in him if not for the obvious fact he batted for the other team.

She wore little makeup. Just a touch of eyeliner and mascara that highlighted eyes that had already stolen his soul.

When she mixed or poured a drink, she tucked the side of her lip under her teeth. What other quirks made up the uniqueness of her?

Colby's co-workers found a seat in the same booth they'd claimed last time. A server had already come over to take orders.

He wanted to talk to her. Even though he suspected another rejection. Being near her, catching her scent, hearing her voice would prove his gluttony for punishment. Given time, maybe he could show her a man worth giving her time to.

"Hey, sugar, bottle of Coors, not light this time." He took a seat on the empty stool on the side of the bar where she'd have to walk away from the crowd to serve him.

When she glanced his way, for a minute he thought he saw pain behind her storm-colored eyes. The look disappeared with a new one of aggravation. He smirked, knowing that look belonged to him.

"You again."

"Me again, baby. Can I get that beer? And a menu."

She reached under the bar and grabbed his beer, popped the cap off, and slid it his way.

"Thanks, darlin'."

"Here's your menu, gramps." A flicker of amusement sparked in her eyes.

Ouch. Gramps? Really. She'd turned their banter into a game. A game he'd gladly play.

Chapter 7

Kenzie

The man whose face and body invaded her dreams for the last month walked back into her bar. If it hadn't been peculiar enough that after one sighting, she'd unintentionally memorized his features with enough detail that she could easily sit down with a sketch artist until he'd drawn a perfect composite. She couldn't even do that for Remy, whom she'd known for more than two decades.

Not for one moment after saving Remy did she regret her sacrifice to keep his happy self around for many more years to come.

The combination of the dreams, and the player sitting in the corner of the bar stealing glances at her definitely planted a seed of longing. She wouldn't call it regret. She'd never wish for another outcome than her best friend's life.

Call it a quiver of desire for something like until-death-do-us-part that would never be hers. The reason she vowed never to fall in love, and the reason why she didn't blink when giving up her sex life for Remy's longevity.

Damn that man. Did he ever turn off that smile? A smile that lit up his dark eyes like fireworks at night.

The name calling grated on her nerves, but she could give as well as take. She could have volunteered her name, but that would only encourage his flirting.

She imagined an interesting story surrounding his younger days. Tattoos decorated both arms—all of females—down to the tops of his hands, and even two four-letter words splashed across his knuckles. One of them she made out when he reached for his beer—h-a-r-d.

A small beauty mole just under his eye begged to be kissed often by someone—other than her.

His salt and pepper beard reminded her of their obvious age difference.

His Bulldogs baseball cap would cause trouble eventually in her Tennessee bar. Had he shaved his whole head for fun or had he lost his hair like many males did with age? Did he wear the hat to hide it, or was he just one of those guys who liked hats?

"Hey, doll, I'm ready to order." The derogatory name shook her. What the hell? *Why am I trying to figure out his life story and what kind of man he is?*

Kenzie walked over without a word and raised her eyebrow. Not in the mood to hold her tongue back from saying something rude—she kept her mouth shut instead.

His grin grew. How the hell? His beauty made her take a step back. Shit. If anyone could tempt her to search for a spell reversal—which, as far as she knew, didn't exist—he would.

"Hamburger and fries, please. And another beer."

"How do you want it cooked?"

"Medium."

Kenzie backed away without losing eye contact. She walked right into Remy.

"Girl, he is fine as hell, but don't knock me down over him."

"I don't know what you're talking about." She spun around and headed to the kitchen to drop his order off with Sylvie.

Remy followed her. "That man crawled under your skin."

"My skin doesn't get crawled under." Kenzie huffed as she handed Sylvie his order.

"Don't sit down because your pants are definitely on fire."

"Kenzie, a customer said there's a man lying on the stairs to the game room. Said he doesn't look right," Joan, one of the servers, popped her head in to inform her.

"You go check. I'll call 9-1-1," Remy volunteered. She loved him to death, but the bravery gene skipped him.

She walked out of the kitchen into a mess

of commotion. A lanky woman grabbed her before she made it to the stairwell. "Where's your AED machine?"

"My what?"

"Portable defibrillator. You're required by law to have one on the premises," she insisted.

Remy came from the back with cell phone in hand and emergency services on the line. Another woman ran up to them, screaming in a panic. "My husband… It's my husband."

Remy shoved the phone in her hand. "Here. It's 9-1-1."

She took the phone from him and ran back to the stairs.

Two young men approached, equally upset. "Did you find the AED?" They asked the lanky female. She looked back at me.

"We don't have one," Kenzie admitted.

"I'll try the businesses next door," one of the men volunteered.

"Sweetheart, can I help?" The man whose presence stirred up so many questions startled her.

"Um, yeah, we need to clear a path for the paramedics. These Nosy Nellies aren't going anywhere, but they need to take a seat." She pointed to the back wall. "There's a microphone over there. Turn the music off and make an announcement. Thanks."

Kenzie took off for the front door. She needed to close up and keep anyone new from entering the premises.

Remy followed her. "We probably need to keep anyone from leaving. What if he was pushed?"

Shit. She hadn't thought of that. "I'll guard the door outside, and you guard the inside."

Kenzie stood outside, waiting for the paramedics. The sirens echoed down the street.

"Where are we headed?" The first responders asked her while grabbing their gear.

She opened the door and pointed in the direction of the stairs and the few individuals standing by the stairs where the man lay.

Kenzie moved out of the way to let the paramedics do their thing. Guard the door, keep others in, or whatever else they needed to do to follow protocol.

<h1 style="text-align:center">Chapter 8</h1>

Colby

Colby made the announcement. His co-workers helped coral the curious onlookers into seats.

He looked around for the bartender, but lost sight of her while handling her request.

She came in from outside, directing the paramedics. She looked pale, and a bit shaken. He made his way to the back of the bar in search of a bottle of water. Colby grabbed the first one he saw and made a beeline for her.

He didn't say anything when he approached. Just handed her the water. She smiled, but it didn't reach her eyes. The beauty drank the whole bottle without taking a breath.

She looked around the bar as if taking in the situation.

Everyone had found a place out of the way, as instructed. Police guarded the doors. Paramedics had disappeared into the stairs—out of sight. The woman screaming it was her husband sat in a corner swaying—alone.

"I'm going to check the cameras. The police will probably want to see them." Her tone—listless.

She didn't invite him to follow her, but he did. Past the kitchen where the employees huddled watching a TV screen with a view of outside the stairs and several other angles of the building. None of which were the stairs themselves.

She looked back at him once she realized he had followed. His heart stopped for a moment, thinking she might send him away. When she turned around and kept walking without a word, relief flooded him.

Colby cared little about being in the know over the situation. His only thoughts were of taking care of her. She acted in charge. Like the situation rested on her shoulders.

On the other side of the kitchen, she entered a small office. It barely fit her desk and chair. With only enough room to maneuver around the desk to have a seat.

A large filing cabinet took up the space behind the door. On top of the filing cabinet sat a TV screen.

His woman took a seat behind the desk, turned the TV on, and moved the cursor around the camera angles. "Shit."

"What's the matter?"

"It's not working."

Colby took a deep breath and walked around the tight space to the side of the desk next to her. He noticed her trembling hands as she pushed the computer mouse around.

He put his hand on top of hers. "Let me. You're shaking."

"I've got to call the insurance company. Uh, this is going to be on the news. What am I going to do?" She rambled without looking at him.

"Let go of the mouse. I'll get it to work."

She relented and sank back into the leather office chair.

A police officer approaching the wife caught both their eyes as they leaned closer to the screen across from them. The smell of her lemon shampoo grazed his nose. He resisted the urge to inhale deeper.

They watched what appeared to be a death notification as the woman stood then crumpled to the floor. Another patron raced to her and helped her back to a seat as she cried those tears no human ever wanted to shed.

He'd left the door open. One of the other workers walked in. "He didn't make it," the woman told them. "The police are looking for the owner."

"Send them back," she told her.

His woman was the owner. Interesting. So young to have her own bar. A popular one at that.

Colby couldn't get the mouse to move around. "Do you have new batteries?"

She leaned over in front of his body to open the drawer. Colby grabbed two from the pack and changed the old ones.

Still nothing.

"Just forget it." She opened the iPad on her desk and went to the camera app. She easily rewound the footage from the device.

"What time do you think it started?" she asked him.

"I believe it was 7:55 when I glanced at my phone."

She zoomed back to 7:40 on the camera in the stairs. He hadn't known the building had a downstairs until the incident.

An officer stepped into the office as they watched the man climb the stairs until he nearly reached the top. He paused briefly before falling face first where he stood without an apparent rhyme or reason.

"Are you the owner?"

"Yes, sir." She didn't stand. Probably because she still looked ready to collapse.

"Can you tell me what happened?"

Colby rested a hand on her shoulder for support while she recanted what she knew, leading up to what they'd just witnessed on the camera.

"Can you show me the footage?"

She rolled back the scene and turned the iPad around for him.

He handed it back to her after watching the tragedy. "His wife said he had a blood clot condition. We don't suspect foul play. Can you send me that footage?" He reached into his pocket for a business card.

"What's your name?"

"Kenzie Wardwell." The officer wrote her sweet name in his notepad he'd been taking notes on.

"Thank you for your help. We're waiting on the coroner. It's still going to be some time before we're finished."

Chapter 9

Kenzie

The touch of another human. She'd forgotten the power behind it. Since her sister's departure, she hadn't experienced a comforting touch. Not a genuine one. Remy used words to express affection.

She hadn't pushed the stranger away because of how much she needed his kind gestures. In another world, she'd have turned around and buried her head in his chest while he held her tight in his arms.

Kenzie had handled a lot of shit over the years on her own, but never someone's death. Despite what the officer told her, she still felt responsible.

To ease her conscience, she did a Google search to verify whether she legally had to keep one of those AED machines in the bar. She sunk back, relieved that only a handful of states had passed that law, and Tennessee wasn't on the list.

She stood up abruptly. "I need to check on the wife. Offer my condolences."

She should ask her comforter for his name, and she probably would have if her brain hadn't been in a state of scramble. He did know her name now.

Kenzie tried to move away from the tight space behind the desk. Only Pops blocked the way. They did the awkward, moving to the same side as each other dance, before he stepped back and out of the room so she could pass.

On her walk back to the front of the bar, she didn't look behind her to watch him follow. She felt his presence lingering at a distance, which brought her a sense of unexpected comfort, only to piss her off that he had that kind of power over her.

Kenzie made her way to the grieving widow sitting at the table, waiting for her husband's body to roll by in a body bag. The lanky female patron sat by her, offering her support.

"Ma'am, I'm Kenzie Wardwell. Owner of *The Witch's Brew.* I'm sorry for your loss. Can I get you anything? On the house."

Through tears and hiccups, "No, thank you."

"If you change your mind, I'll be by the bar."

The widow nodded. Her companion mouthed, "Thank you."

Kenzie needed a seat. Her legs trembled at the strain needed to keep her on her feet. She sat on one of the empty stools.

Remy passed her a water bottle. They

shared an unspoken look of we'll-talk-later.

Mr. Tall Dark Sexy Antique took the empty seat beside her. Remy opened a Coors for him.

She examined him out of the corner of her eye as he picked at the label on the bottle with his thumb.

Words seemed inappropriate with the widow seated thirty feet behind her. An eerie silence hung all across the bar.

She worried about her patrons stuck downstairs. Kenzie reached for the phone in her back pocket to text John.

Kenzie: How is everyone?

John: All good down here. Those who wanted to leave went out the back door. Those sticking around are drinking the situation away.

She'd converted the downstairs basement to a secondary bar not long after she began running *The Witch's Brew* alone. She installed another full bar with a pool table, shuffleboard, darts, a Frogger and a Pac Man machine.

Her bar, like many homes and establishments, had been built tucked into one of the mountains putting the basement not fully underground. Some of her regulars bypassed the front entrance all together and entered through her back door. Business doubled when she added on.

The upstairs served those who wanted food, karaoke, and dancing.

The body bag being pushed out caught her

attention, but she couldn't bring herself to turn around and watch the departed's exit.

Without warning, the silence ended. Time to get back to work. Kenzie pulled herself together and headed behind the bar. She poured herself a shot of Early Times—yeah, her favorite whiskey was bottom shelf whiskey—before serving all those waiting to drink the night away.

Chapter 10

Colby

His co-workers left not long after the dead man had been wheeled out. He stayed behind, fascinated by Kenzie Wardwell's strength and fortitude.

The situation shook her, but who wouldn't experience turmoil during such a tragic moment in their place? She handled herself without falling to a million pieces.

Maybe she would later on her own. A large part of him wanted to be there for her if she did. He had no intention of going anywhere until she basically kicked him out.

Kenzie stayed busy the rest of the night. Not a moment presented itself for him to converse with her or ask her how she was doing.

He hoped she'd let him walk her home when the night ended. She shouldn't have to face it alone. Maybe his heart held out more hope than it should have that she didn't have a man—closer to her age—waiting for her at home.

Someone she couldn't wait to get home to,

so he could fuck her hard until the memories of the night were just that—memories.

A few minutes to midnight rolled around. "Last call." Kenzie shouted loud enough that the few stragglers left could hear without strain.

She pulled another Coors out from under the bar for him. He waved it away. "No thanks. I've had my limit."

He hadn't, but he wanted a clear head on the slim chance she let him walk her home.

The male bartender shoved everyone out the door at midnight on the dot. It puzzled Colby that he didn't ask him to leave, but not enough to question him.

Kenzie approached him. "Pops, it's time to go. I need to close up."

Colby resisted the urge to chuckle when she called him Pops. "I thought I could help."

She turned her head sideways and looked him over. "Isn't it past your bedtime, Gramps?"

"Sweetheart, I can hang all night with you or anyone else, and still get up for my shift in the morning." He should have called her Kenzie, but why stop having fun?

"You can't use the excuse anymore that you don't know my name."

"Why can't I? You haven't officially introduced yourself to me. Overhearing it in conversation doesn't count."

"Fine. *Dude.* You can turn the chairs over onto the tables. If that won't aggravate your aching back.”

Colby chuckled as he handled the task she gave him with joy.

Kenzie's staff worked efficiently closing up for the night. In no time, they had the place ready for the next day. One by one, her employees waved and headed out the door.

“Old Timer, are you still here?”

“I was hoping I could walk you home.”

“Why?”

Before he could answer her, the other bartender pulled her to the side. Colby watched them argue from a distance. He almost imagined the guy argued in his favor.

Chapter 11

Kenzie

"Kenzie, let him be the friend you need tonight," Remy pushed.

"You could do that."

"I need a friend, too. Kelly's waiting for me at home. I'm going to sink into a hot bubble bath with a bottle of wine. You don't need me. You need someone like him."

"It's not fair to him. I can't offer him anything."

"I don't think he's sticking around for sex tonight. Tell him the truth if you must, but don't go upstairs alone. It's not healthy." Remy kissed her cheek and left before she could rebut.

"Well, can I have the honor of walking you home?" Mr. Big asked her. That fit more than all the other names she'd called him so far. Like Mr. Big from *Sex and the City.* She smiled, thinking about all the fights she and Leigh had over Mr. Big and Aiden, Leigh being team Aiden and her being team Mr. Big.

"Fine, Mr. Big, you can walk me home. As a

friend, and nothing more."

"Don't remember asking for anything more."

Smarty pants followed her to the front door and moved to open it for her while she pulled out keys. Kenzie grabbed the door from him and pulled it closed.

"Really, I can't act the gentleman?"

"You can. Except I don't live out there." Kenzie moved to the other door he hadn't paid much attention to beside the bar. "This door you may open."

Mr. Big opened the door she pointed at. His eyes lit up. "Ah, you live here."

"Yes, sir. I have an apartment upstairs, but no one knows that. Except Remy. I get old geezers hitting on me all the time and wouldn't want one thinking he could sneak in and take advantage of me."

"We should settle this. How old are you?" he asked while they climbed the stairs to her place.

"Twenty-six."

"And I'm thirty-eight. I'm not even old enough to be your father."

"Twelve years is still a gap."

"It's not criminal," he defended.

"Um, for twelve years, it was. Like when I was six and you were eighteen."

"We're both adults. That's what matters now—not then."

Kenzie moved aside to allow him to open

her door. She didn't bother apologizing for her mess because, to be fair, she didn't plan to impress him.

"Can I get you a beer, coffee, water?"

"Coffee."

"That won't make you wet the bed, now will it?"

"Miss Priss, I think it's time for proper introductions. Don't you?"

"Why? You're here tonight to be my friend. Nothing more."

"What are you saying? This is a one-night friendship?"

"I can't give you more than that."

"Can't or won't?"

She held her head up in defiance. "Can't."

She pulled a cup of hot coffee from under her Keurig before starting another cup. "Cream, sugar?"

"Just cream."

Kenzie pushed her unopened mail to the side of her kitchen table to make room for the two of them to sit and drink their coffee.

Watching Zeus mix his coffee like he belonged before taking a seat, "If only" ticked in her ears like the heartbeat under the floorboard in *The Tell Tale Heart.*

"How are you holding up?" His kindness only made "If only" scream louder.

"I'm due for a shower and a good cry." Why bother pretending?

"Who holds you when you cry?"

"Who says I need someone to hold me?" She sipped on her coffee mixed with her favorite peppermint mocha creamer. She kept cases of it in her freezer because she never knew when the stores were going to keep it on the shelves. Most of the time marketers deemed it a holiday creamer. What was wrong with peppermint all year long?

"Psychiatrists say it takes seven hugs a day to remain emotionally stable."

"I guess I'm headed for the nuthouse, then."

Mr. Big stood up, grabbed her hand, and yanked her off her seat into his chest. His arms looped around her and pulled her tight into his body. Her imagination didn't do justice to the comfort and security his arms brought her.

Not even thirty seconds went by before the tears fell. She sank deeper into the arms of the man whose name she still didn't know.

Her snot and tears soaked his shirt, and he didn't falter. His hand ran up and down her back. He could have gone lower, and he didn't. He could have ground himself up against her center, and he didn't. He stayed true to their deal of friendship.

Several minutes went by before he scooped her up bridal style and carried her to her bed. Her open floor plan apartment made it easy to find at the back of the room.

Mr. Big laid her down. Took both their shoes off and crawled in beside her before pulling her into his firm body and spooning her.

"Try to get some sleep, Princess. Once you fall asleep, I'll sneak out and leave you to yourself. Until then, I'm here."

Kenzie scooted closer to him. "If only" only shouted louder. In no time, the peace his arms brought her rocked her to sleep.

<h1 style="text-align:center">Chapter 12</h1>

Colby

The walk back to his place had him thinking, and it didn't stop when he went to work the next day. *What does Kenzie mean by can't? Is she married—in the middle of a divorce? Is she married, and he's stationed overseas somewhere? Is she dying?* His imagination had a way of getting ahead of him.

While holding her as friends, it hadn't been appropriate to push the issue. Colby had no intention of giving up. He'd get to the bottom of this *can't* situation sooner rather than later.

Kenzie Wardwell had managed to do what no other woman had ever done before. She'd gotten under his skin, snaked her way through his bloodstream reaching his heart, where she'd woven herself in several directions until rooted deep within. There'd be no way of pulling her out without ripping his heart from his chest in pieces.

"You really not going home with us?" Bryce asked him as he packed his duffle bag.

"Not this time. There's nothing waiting for

me. Go, see your mom. I'll meet you at the job on Monday."

The crew would only go back to Georgia every other weekend. Colby liked the comfort of his own bed, but it didn't feel right to leave Kenzie after the night they'd shared.

Sure, a part of him hoped to grapple his way into her emotions the way she had. He couldn't do that from Macon, Georgia.

"She's got our player whipped after one night." Robert walked by their open door to give his two cents.

Colby ignored the ball busting, slipped his hat on, and headed out the door for the bar.

He took what he'd deemed his newly assigned seat, but didn't see her around.

The male bartender wore the same shirt he'd worn yesterday, just in a different color. "Is Kenzie around?" He tried not to sound desperate.

Kenzie pushed the swinging door to the kitchen open, carrying a basket of wings. She slid them to the young man at the end of the bar before turning to him. "If it isn't my favorite coffin dodger. Coors?"

Coffin dodger. He hadn't heard that term before. She did say he was her favorite—he'd call that a win. He accepted the beer and the menu she set down in front of him.

She left him to peruse the menu while she checked on the young guy with the wings. Colby gritted his teeth when the age-appropriate man grabbed her hand, only to smile when she pulled away from his advances.

While it tempted him to step in, he kept calm. She seemed the type to toss him out the bar and ban him from ever coming back if he involved himself when she had it handled.

He imagined she had lots of practice fending off drunk perverts.

"Wise move, staying in your seat." Her friend noticed his discomfort.

"I'm Colby, Colby Parrish." He stuck his hand out for her companion.

"Jeremiah G. but everyone calls me Remy." He shook his hand in return. "Know what you want?"

"Mind if I wait for Kenzie to take my order?"

Remy chuckled. "Not at all." Remy looked around while Kenzie moved through the room, checking on customers before leaning in toward Colby.

"She won't be won easily. Call her on her bullshit from the start. Make her get real honest right away. Maybe then you'll have a chance."

"Sounds like you're giving me your blessing."

"I've got a good feeling about you."

"I take it she's single."

"Ask her the questions, not me. I won't spill her story, but beware whatever you tell me—I'm telling her."

"Fair enough."

"Trying to steal my customers." Kenzie snuck up on both of them.

"Not me. Never." Remy threw his hands in the air and feigned innocence.

Remy walked away, leaving them on their own. "What can I get you?"

"You can tell me what you meant by *can't.*" He didn't waste a minute taking her friend's advice.

She stepped back. "I meant to eat."

His grin grew, considering her sweet nectar. "Bro, I don't count." She clearly understood where his thoughts were.

"Chicken tenders and fries—for now."

"Men." She huffed on her way to the kitchen.

Chapter 13

Kenzie

She'd pushed "If only" down all day. Just her luck, Mr. Big walked in, bringing it all back up.

Why? Damn it. Why?

She never knew if one big event, like her father's death, had sent her mom over the edge or a bunch of little what ifs. Kenzie imagined someone just like Mr. Big, possibly her dad, had turned her mom into the bastard alcoholic Kenzie spent her life avoiding turning into.

"Why Kenzie sad?" Sylvie asked in broken English when she handed in the orders from the customers. Her best cook may or may not have been undocumented. She didn't ask questions when the hiring company sent over workers. As long as they worked hard and showed up—that's all that mattered to her.

After the last cook walked out in the middle of their shift, Sylvie came in like a breath of fresh air. Remy probably knew her entire life story, but not Kenzie.

Kenzie preferred people to share

information voluntarily, while Remy had a gift for pulling everything about a person out. Don't even get her started on how jealous she felt over his ability to remember the name of everyone who walked in the doors of her bar.

Remy reminded her all the time that they were all made with different gifts. He had none of hers. Together, they made this place a success.

Speaking of Remy, he pushed the revolving door open in a huff. All of her staff wore black t-shirts with a witch's broom logo, but not Remy. He liked to make a statement. His personality left a mark on all who met him, but he didn't consider his habits enough information. Thus, he regularly rebelled and wore a t-shirt warning customers not to mess with his good mood.

He'd never go as far as spitting in someone's drink when they'd pissed him off, but giving them bottom shelf instead of top shelf, more coke instead of alcohol, pouring non-light beer into a light beer bottle, etc. All ways he got back at someone who took the happy out of his night.

"This guy rode in here on his bicycle. When I told him he couldn't come up in here with a bike, he said he'd be back later—to rob me. Uh-uh, I told him to go away with that bicycle, and if he comes back, I'll be waiting for him.

"He was fine, too. Did you see him? Uh huh, I need a new pen pal. Cause that's all he's going to get out of me if he comes back up in here to take our money.

"Dear Mr. Robber, here's five bucks. Buy yourself something nice while in prison."

Remy turned and walked away without waiting for anyone to respond. The kitchen staff cackled at his story. Kenzie had grown accustomed to his rants, but they never ceased to bring a smile to her face.

She'd come into the kitchen to hide from Mr. Big. Not two seconds after Remy made his dramatic exit, he peeked his head back in. "Am I taking care of your brown-eyed demi-god tonight, or are you coming back out?"

Kenzie swallowed the urge to further dampen Remy's mood, telling him with several choice words how she felt about his meddling. His actions made no sense. Her best friend knew her secrets, knew her pain, knew what she'd sacrificed. Until Mr. Big, she believed Remy believed her history. He'd never acted like he doubted her before. Now, not so much. She didn't know what to think. Why had he suddenly done a one-eighty like none of her limitations mattered?

Her head told her to find a hole to bury itself in, yet her feet took her back out to the bar.

Another day of dreaded interviews. Anyone who worked for her made decent money, so it always baffled her that people didn't stick around longer.

Kenzie didn't consider herself difficult to

work for. She put in the same shift hours as everyone else, if not more, on top of the extra hours she worked in the office.

No one could accuse her of being an absent boss. She rarely nagged. Her employees could just about ask her for anything—she rarely said no.

They still all left. She called herself lucky when an employee stuck around for more than six weeks. And she did have several on staff who'd been with her for the last year. She made sure to let them know how much she appreciated them on a regular basis.

Having a permanent team working under her would make life so much simpler. Every small business owner's dream.

The first guy she interviewed had track marks on his arms and most of his teeth had fallen out. If she needed a dishwasher, she might have been desperate enough to give him a chance, but she couldn't give him the server position she needed filled. Customers tend to not come back if they are worried the individual bringing them food has a drug problem.

Her next three interviews were no shows. She expected that. Kenzie didn't understand making an appointment for an interview and not showing up, but more people stood her up than actually walked in her doors ready to work.

She'd nearly given up for the day when her last applicant walked in ten minutes late for the interview. Late—never a good sign.

Kenzie looked at her list to refresh her memory on the young woman's name. Jamie. Jamie Moses.

Kenzie offered her hand to Jamie in her inappropriate red halter top, black miniskirt, fishnet stockings, and black high heels. All things she should never have left the house in, as they accented every fat roll on her body. And there were several. Jamie accepted her hand and shook it. The woman's touch gave Kenzie an eerie feeling. Waves of warning washed through her gut. She pulled her hand away and resisted the urge to scrub her palm with the nearest towel.

"I'm Kenzie Wardwell. You must be Jamie."

"Ye-s." Jamie barely got the word out before hacking her lungs up in a fit. The woman didn't bother to cover her mouth as she spread her germs on Kenzie and all the surfaces near them.

Kenzie smelled alcohol on her breath. Had she been drinking before lunch?

Jamie awkwardly pulled an inhaler from her cleavage. The issue of her day drinking momentarily forgotten. Her rolls bounced as she shook the device before putting her pasted red lips on the mouthpiece. One deep inhale and exhale later, she had herself under control. Kenzie's mouth dropped as she watched Jamie wipe the lipstick off the inhaler with the bottom of her halter top. The skin underneath her shirt fell over her skirt. The woman pushed her inhaler back down the crease of her breasts before tucking her belly back into her top.

Kenzie shook her head—miffed that the options for employees lately were slim pickins'.

"Have a seat. Please."

Jamie pushed her thick-lensed, saucer-sized glasses up and took the seat at the two-seater table.

At least she had all her teeth and no track marks. She'd probably even pull in males who had a thing for plus size girls.

"Have you ever waited tables before?"

"Yes, back home. I just moved here from Minnesota. I worked in a place similar to this one for the last six years."

"Do you have a problem wearing a uniform?" It relieved Kenzie that Jamie wouldn't be able to prance around in her inappropriate attire while on the job.

"Do you have anything I can snack on? I missed breakfast trying to find this place." Jamie rudely stood up without answering Kenzie's question and walked over to the bar. Her ankle twisted. She had no grace in her blunder to recover her footing. Yep, definitely a bit tipsy. The woman grabbed the bag of mini pretzel twists Kenzie set out earlier to use for filling the bowls.

Jamie plopped back down, opened the bag without waiting for permission, and grabbed a handful. She shoved three into her mouth all at once.

"I'll wear your uniform." Pretzel crumbs flew from her mouth as she spoke before chewing her food and swallowing.

Kenzie regretted it before she even said it. "Can you start tonight?"

Chapter 14

Colby

Colby stood outside the bar and lit up his first cigarette in his second pack of the night. A damn nasty habit he went back and forth with. He hadn't had a cigarette in nine months.

He woke up covered in semen in the middle of the night and couldn't go back to sleep. The last wet dream he had, he'd still been a virgin. Those dreams were nothing compared to what he just experienced.

He could still feel Kenzie's lips wrapped around his cock. Like a genuine memory, and not a fucking dream. Who has dreams powerful enough to leave the sensation behind? Not him. Not ever. It left him freaked. The word *bewitched* came to mind again.

She held a power over him like none other. Common sense told him he should find another place to spend his evenings. Yet there he stood, giving himself a peptalk to get his feet and legs to take him inside—to her.

Colby's thoughts consumed him so much,

he didn't hear someone walk up beside him. "I didn't know you smoked."

He turned to see Remy lighting up his own cigarette beside him while he bounced from the bitter chill.

"Nine months. Damn it. That's the longest I've ever quit. It's her fault. She's bewitched me. I just know it." The words vomited from his lips to her best friend's ear. Damn it. Remy warned him he'd tell Kenzie anything he said about her.

"Kenzie is powerful, but she cannot steal your free will." Remy's words only added to his confusion.

Colby tossed the butt of the cigarette into the nearby ashtray. He'd inhaled it until nothing but the tip remained. He pulled another one out and struggled to light it, since the wind turned to blow in his direction.

"She hates cigarettes. Just so you know."

"You smoke," Colby defended himself.

"True, but I have no intention of kissing her *anywhere*."

Colby furrowed his brows. "Why do you care?"

Remy took a deep drag and exhaled before answering him. "Kenzie deserves a happy ending. Right now, she can't have one. But I have a feeling that's about to change."

"What does that mean? She can't have a happy ending?"

"You'll have to ask her." Remy put his arm

around Colby's shoulder. "Colby, I like you. Two other times in my twenty-six years, did I get this nagging feeling. Like someone whispering in my ear incessantly. It never shuts up.

"I was six. I'd just moved in next door to Kenzie and her family. It took me a year of watching her playing outside with her sister before I listened to the nagging and befriended her. Best decision of my life.

"I was twenty-three when I heard it again. Like a buzzing sound. I didn't feel sick. I didn't act sick. No signs, but I knew I needed to get to a doctor right away. Stage four colon cancer. I wouldn't be here today if I ignored that knowing.

"It's the same with you. Neither one of you knows it yet, but you're everything she believed she could never have. You'll see."

Remy put his cigarette out and walked away. Colby lit up another. Common sense won the night's argument as he turned and headed back to the house.

Colby stayed away for three nights. The longest three nights of his life. Each of those nights he had a similar dream, only to wake each time covered in a sticky hot mess.

He'd switched to only cold showers.

His need to be near Kenzie wouldn't let him hide from her for another night.

Chapter 15

Kenzie

Kenzie huffed. "Dude, why are you staring at me?" She tossed the bar towel on the ground, ready to turn and storm off. Her admirer's attention scraped against her nerves like a rash on a hot summer's day. She didn't need this.

"I always stare at you."

She rolled her eyes. "Tonight it's different." She couldn't put her finger on it, but the look he gave her *did* seem different from his usual one-day-I'm-going-to-fuck-you look.

He leaned forward, his elbows rested on the bar top. "It's your eyes. Tonight they are haunted."

Something about the concern seeping from his tone made Kenzie lean in on the bar. She always made a point to stay as far away from him as possible. Never getting close enough that he could touch her.

"It's just one of those days. We all have days that remind us of how shitty our lives are. Today's one of mine."

"Life dealt you a nasty hand. Please, tell me

how yours compares to the rest of ours."

Kenzie stood back up. Offended by his words, but deep down she knew he meant no offense by them. It didn't stop her from going off as she vomited her "nasty hand."

She picked up the towel from the floor and wrung it between her hands. This man had a way of getting under her skin—like a bad splinter.

"Where should I begin? Oh, right. How about the fact that I'm a witch who can trace her ancestors all the way back to Salem? That I've been taught my whole life about the spell my ancestor cast for another family. Oh wait, did I mention that spells come at a price? And hers came at a steep price. She sacrificed our happily ever afters. We are all doomed to heartache and pain until one of my relatives falls in love with a descendant from the family she spelled. No idea who or when that might happen. It's only been three centuries.

"Then there's my mom, right? Just like so many other Wardwell women who gave into the desire for love and attention, she fell for my dad. Everything went fine at first. Moved in together. Had two girls. Then, out of nowhere, she comes home from the bar. My sister and I are in our beds screaming. We're only three and one. Where's my dad? I'll tell you where my dad is. He's sitting in his favorite chair in the living room with a shotgun in his hand and half his face blown off.

"Instead of going to therapy or talking to her sisters, she turns to the bottle. Of course, her never-ending supply—" Kenzie motioned around the room "—only kept her habit going.

"I don't remember my dad, but I remember my mom. Drunk—every day of my life.

"Well, my sister, my friend, decides she's had enough at fourteen and walks out the door. Won't answer my calls. No idea where she is. Nothing.

"Dear old mom just gets drunker. Not long after my twenty-first birthday, she leaves here—wasted. Got in her car—like she always did and drove intoxicated. Only this time, she didn't make it home. Nope—killed an entire family. She's where she belongs—locked up.

"And that's only part of the shitty hand life dealt me."

Out of breath, she wished for a chair to fall into.

The man she spilled her guts to stood up to lean over the counter, grabbed the towel in her hand, and pulled her closer to him.

"Breathe, baby. What happened today to get you all riled up?"

Kenzie looked at him, perplexed. Usually, when she mentioned being a witch, questions got tossed at her. *If only* took the place of all the day's pain as she surprised herself by answering his question. How did he do that? He could get her to tell him anything.

"Mommy dearest is up for parole. She sent me a letter asking me to come speak on her behalf."

While staring into her eyes with his damn sparkly ones, "Hey, Remy, you got the night covered?" he shouted behind her without breaking eye contact.

"I'm all good," Remy assured them.

"Are you any good at pool? I hear there's a table downstairs."

Damn those eyes and that smile. *If only.*

Chapter 16

Colby

Kenzie had dumped a lot of information in his lap all at once. She didn't say anything that made him want to bolt out the door, though.

He did have questions. Lots of them, but thought it better to wait to ask them. Like when her emotions weren't so overloaded.

When he suggested pool, he thought the distraction would do them both some good.

Colby escorted her down the stairs with his hand on the small of her back. He smiled when her body visibly trembled when he made contact with the curve that fit the palm of his hand perfectly.

A group of four occupied the table, so they took a seat on stools in the corner to wait their turn.

"Are you any good?" he asked her.

Their eyes met when she turned her head to look at him. She smiled. Something he rarely saw her do. He longed to bring her a reason to keep the beautiful smile on her face.

"I grew up in a bar. Of course, I'm good."

A high-pitched squeal made them both turn. "I knew I'd find you here." His gut dropped to his feet, as he recognized his failed fuck from over a month ago. She threw her arms around his neck. Colby didn't reciprocate. He looked like a deer in headlights. Why in the world did the slut he walked out on find excitement in seeing him again? What did she mean when she said she knew she'd find him here?

Colby pried her arms from around his neck and pushed her away. "What's the matter, baby? Aren't you happy to see me?" She poked her lip out in a pout.

She looked like the same woman he went home with, but she acted like a totally different person.

"Jamie, you two know each other?" Kenzie asked her. The hurt in her voice—unmistakable.

"Of course, he's my bae and I'm his sugar muffin." Colby stifled the urge to vomit. He jumped to his feet in defense.

"Are you drunk?" Her foul breath hit him in the face. Alcohol laced with vomit made him want to puke. "Jamie, is it? What's my name?" He grabbed Kenzie's wrist when she moved to leave him.

"You're my bae."

"Bae is Danish for shit. I'm nobody's shit." Through gritted teeth, he demanded, "What's my name?"

Jamie stomped her foot. "I came all this

way to be with you. Why are you treating me this way? I don't have to stand here and take this." She stormed off, but not without tripping over a chair.

Colby hung his head and refused to look at Kenzie. He hadn't let go of her wrist. His heart skipped with hope, as she hadn't pulled away from him, either. "We had a few drinks. She invited me back to her place. We never even exchanged names. She's bat shit crazy." Kenzie moved to walk away from him. He didn't hold on to her. He had no right to.

"Are you racking, or am I?" The table had opened up during the commotion. He turned to see her with a stick in one hand with the other on her hip.

She's going to be the death of me.

Chapter 17

Kenzie

"What did he see in *her?*" She slammed the chair she'd lifted onto the table while closing up for the night.

"Her? Who? I need more details," Remy pushed.

"Apparently, Gramps had a one-night stand with Jamie."

"Your Gramps? Recently? I'll kill him." His chair fell harder on the table he set it on. Everyone else had clocked out and gone home, leaving just the two of them to clean up. She preferred it that way. Idle chat with anyone other than Remy only added to the exhaustion of a long night.

"Calm down. It happened before he started following me around like a puppy dog. She threw herself all over him, like they were old lovers. Called him her bae."

Remy laughed. "I'm not seeing Gramps as a bae."

"She couldn't even tell him his real name when he asked her for it. She just kept pouting and calling him bae. Apparently, bae is Danish for shit, which he pointed out to her. I wanted to laugh so hard when he said that to her."

"Do you know his name yet?"

"No."

"I could tell you."

Kenzie shook her head. "He remains nameless. If I know his name… I just can't." She couldn't put into words what knowing his name would mean to her. A name to wish she could change hers to. A name to scream out when she woke from a nightmare. A name to remember when he walked out of her life for good.

"Did you fire Jamie?" Remy knew just how to handle her when he changed the subject.

She tilted her head. A wicked gleam sparkled in her eyes. "I pictured firing her. Then I imagined the workforce commissioner asking for the reason for her termination. 'Well, sir, I just didn't like her. Or she came on to the man I can't have. Or she got under my skin.' The fine for unjustifiable termination is more than I can afford.

"I still don't get it. What did he see in her? She's foul, a drunk, and has no manners."

"I'm no expert, but I've seen her with the customers. They all like her. She's got curves in all the right places that straight men find appealing."

Kenzie stared at Remy, confusion written across her forehead. Curves in all the right places. Was that what it was called these days?

"The men probably like her because her

inebriated self-flirts with all of them."

"He only has eyes for you, so what are you worried about?"

A tear cascaded down her cheek. "He'd be better off turning his eyes back to her."

"Nope, don't do that." Remy wiped the tear from her eye. "I'm certain this curse is going to be broken in *your* lifetime. I just know it."

If only.

"Even if that's true—I still can't have him." She shuffled her feet along the stained cement floor on her way to the door leading to her room. The rest of the cleanup could wait till morning.

"Once I finish with these chairs, I'll bring you a hot toddy," Remy called after her.

Chapter 18

Colby

"Bae, what can I get you?" *I can't hit a woman. I can't hit a woman.*

Colby turned to the nutcase and plastered a smile on his face. "I'm not your bae. You need to stop calling me that."

His request went unheeded as she pressed herself up against him. The scoop she'd cut out of her uniform shirt pushed her breasts up for all to see. Before Kenzie, he'd without a doubt have enjoyed the picture in front of him.

I can't hit a woman. He took a deep breath. "Jamie, please go bother someone else."

Her smile grew wider. "You remembered my name. See, you are my bae." She jerked her head while departing, her hair caught in his eye, causing it to pool with water. Cray cray needed her medication. A woman that nutty had to be on something. Alcohol alone couldn't make a woman that nutty.

"Jamie! What are you doing up here?" The raising of Kenzie's voice caught Colby off guard.

"I switched shifts with Tracy." She batted her eyes at Kenzie like she thought her good looks would manipulate her boss.

"Remy, get Tracy up here now."

"What? I didn't think you'd mind." Colby rolled his eyes. The innocent act hadn't fooled anyone.

"Let me make myself clear. I'm the boss. I have my reasons for who I assign upstairs and downstairs. You—the employee—do not get to switch things up without my or Remy's say so. Do I make myself clear?"

Jamie tossed her hands in the air. "Fine. Whatever you say."

She marched down the stairs in a huff.

The other poor woman walked back in with Remy. "I'm sorry. I didn't know. I didn't mind switching."

"I mind" is all Kenzie told her in a much calmer voice than the one she used on Jamie.

Colby smiled. Whether true or not, he imagined Kenzie jealous and that she'd put Jamie downstairs to keep her away from him.

It surprised him that Kenzie didn't fire her for being a drunk. He considered bringing it up, but he chose to mind his own business for now. If she got worse or acted dangerous, he wouldn't hold his tongue.

Colby finished the last bite of his steak. Kenzie grabbed his plate and placed another beer in front of him. She didn't have to ask what he wanted. They'd developed a pattern.

More often than not, she avoided looking at him. In those moments when she did lock eyes with him, he made sure she could see the longing for more in his eyes.

He leaned back on his stool. With his hands on his belly, he asked her. "Baby, If I asked you to rub my belly, what would you say?"

She looked at him like he'd just spit in her gravy. Kenzie rolled her head before walking away with his dirty dishes.

Remy gave him a did-you-really ask-her-that look.

"What? I like my belly rubbed after a heavy meal."

Before Remy could tell Colby what he really thought about asking a woman for a belly rub, the melody of Kenzie's voice captured their attention.

Not just their attention. Everyone on the floor stopped talking and gave her their undivided gaze.

A young couple danced in each other's arms as Kenzie sang the words to "When a Man Loves a Woman" originally sung by Percy Sledge. While Michael Bolton's version held more power, his voice hadn't the emotion behind it to enrapture each soul.

Again, tears slipped from Colby's eyes. He held on tight to his seat. His knuckles clutched the chair as his body tugged at him to pull her from the piano and show her the true meaning of a man loving a woman.

"Damn, Colby."

It took his brain a moment to catch up to Remy's comment.

"What?" Colby stared at Kenzie. Her head hung as if exhausted after the song ended. No one applauded. All too moved to disturb the tangible power her voice brought to the atmosphere.

Out of the corner of his eye, he noticed Remy rest his elbows on the counter. "You do that to her."

"What?" Colby turned to give Remy his full attention.

"I know you heard her say she's a witch. You probably blew it off as just talk. It's not talk. It's true. One of her gifts is the ability to feel the emotions of the songwriter and/or of the one requesting the song. It takes a toll on her. She rarely agrees to sing. You were here the last time she performed, too."

"What does that matter?"

"I think your emotions or her feelings. Or maybe both are coupled with the requester's feelings. It's never been this powerful."

"You can't be serious. She barely tolerates me."

"It's just a theory," Remy practically whispered.

Colby turned back to the piano. Kenzie's head rested on the top. He stood, worried.

"Usually, she just needs a few moments to

recover. Last time I had to carry her up to her room and put her to bed."

Colby took her friend's words to mean she'd need help again, and he wanted to be the one to take care of her.

Chapter 19

Kenzie

What the hell is happening to me? Tired. I'm so tired.

Her head fell to the piano. Moments later, strong arms lifted her off the bench. The smell of stale cigarettes made her think of Remy. He never picked her up in his arms. Her eyes wouldn't open to check.

She let her head rest on his shoulder. His arms felt like home. Even better than her sister's comfort touch. Something only a sibling witch could do. They could enhance the comfort they offered each other tenfold in just a touch. Oh, how she missed Leigh.

Leigh would get a kick out of Mr. Big. She'd act like she hated him for using derogatory names all the time. Yet she'd secretly enjoy the way he got under Kenzie's skin.

Her rescuer laid her on her bedsheets and tucked her in. Her mouth wouldn't open to form the words, *don't go.* He grabbed her hand and gave it a gentle goodbye squeeze. Kenzie squeezed tighter. Refusing to let go. It was all the strength she could muster.

"Kenzie, you need to let go so you can rest."

Is that Mr. Big? Did he call me Kenzie? He likes me. If only. She held onto his hand tighter.

"Kenzie, sweetheart, are you asking me to stay?"

She tightened her grip on his hand.

"I'm taking that as a yes, beautiful. Damn the consequences."

His body sunk her mattress in deeper. His arms wrapped around her as he pulled her into his warm embrace. *We're going to have to talk about the cigarettes. Has he always smoked?*

Kenzie woke to the smell of fresh coffee brewing. Startled, she sat up straight in her bed. *Why am I wearing my clothes from last night?*

She looked across the apartment. Mr. Big sat at her tiny kitchen table, looking at his phone with a cup of coffee in his hand.

It all came back to her. She sang that stupid song. It drained her more than usual. Leaving her feeling like she'd had one too many edibles. He carried her to bed, and she begged him not to leave.

Ugh, what did I do? She fell back onto her pillow. *Maybe he'll go away, and we can pretend this never happened. If only.*

"Would you like a cup of coffee? It's hot." Damn. He'd noticed she'd awoken.

Kenzie sat up to face the music. *He's going to think I want him. Of course, I want him. I just can't have him. Shit, double shit. Just shit.*

When did he take my shoes off? Her bare feet touched the cold floor. *I really should get a rug for under my bed.*

Their eyes met. He gave her that stupid smile that would set a normal woman's lady bits on fire. *If only.*

"Remy tells me you really are a witch."

Now he wants to talk about that. "I did tell you that the other night."

He nods. "You did."

Kenzie joined him at the table. "Cream right?" She watched him pour her creamer in her cup first before filling it with coffee. She shut her hanging mouth before he turned around. He paid attention. *Great, more reasons to be likeable. Just shoot me now.*

Mr. Big handed her the cup. The warmth of the hot liquid on the outside of the cup felt heavenly. They must have fallen asleep without the heater.

"What do you want to know?" She hid behind the coffee mug. Time to lay it all out there for him. Be done with it, so they can both move on.

"Is it like a wiccan thing that I've read about? Or more like the witches in movies?"

Kenzie lifted her legs into her chest, holding them tight, thinking it might give her the courage she needed. Remy knew everything about her.

Being a witch didn't have to be a secret anymore. They were no longer in danger of being burned or hung from a noose. It was the twenty-first century. Anybody could be anything without fear of death.

"It always starts with evil. A lone individual seeks power. Seeks the unnatural. The father of shadows is only too happy to grant them powers that come from him. As long as they use it to create havoc and chaos. The one who petitioned the father of shadows condemns their descendants to the same fate.

"The universe always finds a way to keep a balance. The father of light finds a willing, worthy individual and offers them abilities to counter the evil. When a wicked witch is formed, a good one emerges. And their descendants are tasked with cleaning up after the evil ones."

"And you are a good witch?" he asked her.

Kenzie nodded her head. "My family has been fighting our enemies for over three hundred years."

"And there really were witches in Salem?"

"There were. Only one true witch hanged from the gallows. All the others were innocent. And witchcraft wasn't even the cause of the panic. That's a long story for another time."

Mr. Big grabbed her hand. She told herself to pull away, but she couldn't. The peace filled her like a drug. Like an addict who knows it's bad for them, but has to have it, anyway.

"Something haunts you. I can see it in your

eyes. Is it your enemy? What is it?"

"I haven't been assigned to stop a Somes witch—that's their name. One hasn't crossed my path."

"Then what is it? What keeps you up at night?"

"Magic is never free. Even good magic. It always requires an offering." She stopped. Hoping he wouldn't press her, but knowing her hopes were for nothing.

"Go on."

"In Salem, my ancestor, she cursed my family."

"How bad can it be?"

"Wardwell women will never have a happily ever after—with a man—until the curse is broken."

"Why would she curse her own descendants? It can be broken, though. How?"

"She made a sacrifice to gift a family that has lasted for generations. An offering that has turned into a curse. One of our own making.

"The curse will break when one from that family falls in love with a Wardwell."

"Sounds like we need to have a matchmaking party with your family and theirs."

Kenzie laughed. "It has to be fate. It doesn't matter for me. I'll never have a happily ever after, even if the curse is broken in my lifetime."

"That's just fear talking."

"I made an offering of my own."

Mr. Big leaned back in his chair. His hand

fell from hers. She couldn't look at him.

"I'd do it again. My reasons for doing what I did. They were worth it."

In a whisper, he asked her. "What did you offer?"

"My ability to get aroused." *There, I said. It's out there. Let him run and never look back.*

Chapter 20

Colby

The skeptic in him wanted to laugh at her confessions. The knife in his heart and the sinking feeling in his gut sang a different tune. How he knew baffled him, but he knew she hadn't made any of it up.

Careful, Colby, what you say and do next might just be the most important thing you ever do.

Words twisted through his mind like a vine raveling through a garden. *Am I man enough to love a woman without sex? Is sex all that matters to me? Am I willing to walk away because I might never feel her pussy squeeze my dick?*

Colby gently took her chin and lifted her eyes to look at him.

"What if I or someone else came into your life, rocked your world, became the air that you breathe—only they were paralyzed and couldn't perform?"

Her mouth dropped. She sat speechless.

"I mean it, Kenzie. Sex isn't the only thing that makes a relationship."

She stood up and pushed her chair in. Her coffee long forgotten and cold, she dumped it in the sink.

Colby moved behind her and pinned her to the counter. She sank back into him. "What do you feel right now?" His arms wrapped around her and pulled her closer to his chest.

"Peace."

He moved the hair from the nape of her neck and kissed the tender spot. "And now?"

"Comfort."

She turned around to face him. Tears slid from both eyes.

"I think whoever said 'It's better to have loved and lost than to have never loved at all' knew what they were talking about," he told her.

She took a deep breath, closed her eyes, and let out a tortuously long exhale before pushing away from him.

"Are you telling me that you'd give up fucking for someone you barely know?"

Colby opened his mouth to respond, but she cut him off. "What about when your dick is hard as a rock, and I have nothing to offer you? No reprieve. When your balls are painfully blue? I mean, I guess I could lie there and just let you have your way. What about then, when I'm dry as a bone, and your dick is rubbing me raw? When the look in my eyes begs for you to hurry up and finish? How about the first time you see me naked and know that your touch won't send shivers down my spine? That it won't make me beg for you to take me, to own me, to fill me. That I'll never scream out your name in ecstasy. That my legs won't tremble from the many orgasms you're equipped to give a woman."

She looked down at his crotch. Her head titled to the side. "Even now, just a conversation about sex has made your dick press against your zipper. What kind of life is that?"

"It's a life you don't get to decide for me. I make my own choices, and damn it, Kenzie, I want you. Any way that I can have you."

Colby turned to leave. He spoke to her with his back to her. "I'm not running. You're the only one running. I'm walking out this door to give you time to think about us. About what I'm offering."

Chapter 21

Kenzie

Kenzie crawled back out of her bed she'd climbed into to wallow in self-pity after Mr. Big left her that morning.

She dragged her heavy body down the stairs to open the bar. Her employees walked about as if the world continued to spin on its axis, while her world had come to a halt.

The man whose name she still hadn't bothered to ask for basically declared his intentions and said to hell with the consequences. Could she do the same? Could she open her heart for a temporary epic love story? One doomed to fail, but one to remember as she grew old alone.

Remy had the news on the TV behind the bar. He always had it on before opening time. She preferred to only turn it on for her patrons when one of Tennessee's teams played. Even then, she kept the volume on mute. If patrons wanted to watch all the games that aired, they had to go downstairs for that.

"The third murder-suicide in the last week

has Knoxville detectives asking whether these incidents are really murder-suicides or simply staged to look that way."

Her mother's teachings hadn't prepared her. Not even close. Wave after wave of terror, fear, anger, and pure evil spun in circles around her body like a cyclone locking her feet in place.

Her eyes sank into the back of her skull. Her hands froze by her side. If only she could move them, she could push through the barrier enclosed around her.

A foghorn, sirens, screeching, and more all pierced her ears.

She was barely aware of the two men on each side of her, each lifting her up under her arms. They carried her with feet dangling to the back office.

Not now. Why now?

As quickly as her assignment captured her, it released her with the same haste. With no regard for where she stood or who stood beside her, her feet fell from underneath her, unprepared for the sudden freedom from their temporary prison.

Mr. Big and Remy both raced to help her up. Remy relinquished his hold as Mr. Big maneuvered her into the limited space behind her desk.

"Was that it?" Remy asked her in a panic.

"Water," she whispered. Her voice cracked from the fire burning her esophagus.

"Is someone going to tell me what just happened?" Mr. Big's worry tugged at her heart.

Damn heart. Damn Somes. I don't need this. Not right now.

Kenzie drank both bottles of water Remy handed her.

"The murder-suicides—it's a Somes."

Remy nodded his head in understanding while Mr. Big crossed his arms and looked at her like I'm-going-to-need-more-information.

"It's like a built-in alarm system. When a Somes is causing havoc near a Wardwell, the closest Wardwell is activated to find her and stop her."

"How often does this happen?"

"My first time."

"Can we help?" Mr. Big generously offered.

"Uh-uh, not me. I'm out. You know I love you, girl, but nope. Just nope. I'm going to go check on the staff. Make sure someone unlocked the door."

Remy left the room as if his ass had caught fire.

"Don't judge him. Darkness, death, anything paranormal, he doesn't handle it very well. He hates going down the stairs since the man died on them. And don't get him started on the ghost he believes haunts the bar."

"A ghost. Really? Um, do ghosts exist? I mean, before yesterday, I thought witches were hocus pocus."

Kenzie smiled. "I honestly don't know if ghosts are real or not."

"What about vampires or werewolves?"

She laughed a hearty laugh. "No idea. And before you ask about other mythological creatures, I'll say the same thing. No idea."

"Back to this Somes person. What can I do?"

"Nothing." She pursed her lips and crossed her arms.

"There's got to be something I can do to help."

"Right now, I have to find her. She's most certainly cloaked herself, so I won't be able to scry for her. I'll have to gain access to the police reports. I'm not a hacker, so I'll have to put together a spell to get them."

"Won't that require another offering?"

"It's part of it. That's my life."

"What if I know a hacker? You can save your offerings for something else."

"You know a hacker?"

He took his cap off and rubbed his head. She'd never seen him without it. He looked sexier without the hat. She kept her mouth shut about it. No need to encourage his affections.

The Somes took priority over anything else.

"It's his side gig. You'd probably have to hire him. I've never seen him work for free."

"And he'd just hack into police records? No questions asked?"

"He's my roommate. I've never hired him before, but he's tightlipped about those who pay him."

"How expensive is he?" Money didn't matter, she had more than she could spend in her lifetime. Between the money her family made on their luck potion and her investments, she could pay any fee. But on principal, she wouldn't let someone cheat her.

Mr. Big pulled his phone out. "Can I text him and ask for you?"

Kenzie nodded.

Chapter 22

Colby

She hadn't told him to get lost. He took that as a good sign.

She even sank into his touch and sighed when he cupped her cheek before they went back to the bar.

He ate the burger she brought him and sipped on his beer while he watched her work the room. Most everyone who stopped by *The Witch's Brew* were regulars, and they all loved her.

Remy's hospitable personality brought new customers back a second and third time, but her warm spirit turned them into permanent fixtures. She didn't give herself enough credit.

Colby overheard more than one conversation between her and Remy. Kenzie wanted to emulate the fun, easygoing attitude Remy gave to everyone. She praised him regularly and never hid her jealousy.

"Crazy woman, nine o'clock," Remy warned him as Jamie headed their way.

"Jamie. What are you doing upstairs?"

Kenzie stood behind the wacko with her hands on her hips, fury radiating off her.

"Joan asked to switch. Ask her." Jamie pointed at Joan walking out of the kitchen with several baskets of wings lining her arms.

"Ask me what?"

"Did *you* ask Jamie to switch positions with you tonight?" Colby noticed Kenzie worded the question to match Jamie's claims.

Joan scrunched her brow in confusion. "You know, I don't remember how it happened. One minute I'm waiting tables up here and the next I'm down there."

"Joan, drop your wings off and come back to your station up here."

Kenzie got in Jamie's face while she wagged her finger at the woman. "Downstairs or go home. Your choice."

Kenzie turned on her heels. Jamie gave her boss the finger behind her back on her way to the basement.

Bryce slapped him on the shoulder, taking his attention away from the brunette whom he'd tear the world apart for—if only she'd let him in. Curse be damned.

If he could only love her with his entire being for a day, it would be more bearable than the pain of never loving her.

He never understood the scenario of leaving someone before they hurt you. Bull shit. Face that hurt when it happens, and cling tight to what you have while you have it.

"Tell me more about this job."

Bryce took a seat next to him. His co-worker and roommate for the last couple of years had to be fourteen years his junior. He stood no more than five-foot, four. Just as rough around the edges as Colby, especially when either of them had too much to drink. He still had that baby face with fine patches of stubble, waiting for the last umph of hormones to kick in and thicken it out.

Kenzie dropped off a beer for each of them before she went back to her other customers.

"You probably won't believe a word I tell you, but I need you to do the job anyway."

"Sounds mysterious. I'm in."

Colby told him all he knew. Except the parts about Kenzie's offering and the family curse.

Chapter 23

Kenzie

After closing up the bar, she climbed the stairs to where she allowed another man to know where she laid her head at night.

Mr. Big and his friend had gone up to her apartment a couple of hours ago to set up the computers and search the Knoxville police records.

She hadn't talked to her great Aunt Willow in years. They were never close. Aunt Willow had the sight, and she knew she'd need to call her soon for advice. She'd be able to look into the future for the Somes' next victims.

Kenzie wanted more information before she called Aunt Willow. Kenzie didn't understand all the rules of their craft, but she accepted them. Using Aunt Willow's ability to find victims and stop a Somes didn't require an offering. Something she could feel grateful for in this nightmare thrust upon her.

Just outside her door, the smell of fresh coffee made her pause. She could never get enough of the delicious aroma. She inhaled deeply and allowed the calm it brought her to seep through her.

For as little time as she and Mr. Big spent together, he knew her better than he should have.

If only she could come home every night to someone waiting for her. She had always believed it would have been Leigh and her—old maids till the end. Now she prayed she'd at least hear from her again in this life.

Her heart skipped a beat when she walked into her apartment to see the two of them sitting on her couch, hunched over two laptops. Weird—how could *both* of them give her a sense of rightness?

She shook the feeling off for another day. They had work to do. Coffee first.

Kenzie grabbed a kitchen chair and her favorite coffee mug Remy gave her on her last birthday. *I hope we're friends until we die. Then I hope we stay ghost friends and walk through walls and scare the shit out of people.*

The guys hadn't seemed to notice her. They were glued to the computer screens. She set the chair down next to the sofa. Her ugly brown couch with wooden arms rests, which she'd found on the side of the road, seated three people, but the idea of sitting so close to either man made her anxious.

Mr. Big looked up. His smile that lit up his melt-in-your-mouth chocolate eyes made her sip her hot coffee too fast, burning the top of her mouth.

His friend stood up and put his hand out. "I'm Bryce, you must be Kenzie."

Kenzie shook his hand. She didn't want to let go at first. His touch reminded her so much of Leigh's. She looked down at his hand in confusion. Bryce took his hand back, reminding her of the emptiness she felt inside.

Mr. Big cleared his throat. She glanced his way. A look of sadness had taken the place of his beautiful smile. He stood up. "You sit here so you can see what Bryce has found."

They switched seats. Kenzie willed her arm to stay by her side as they passed each other while switching positions. She refused to give into the urge to grab his hand and give him a reassuring look that her moment with Bryce didn't mean what he thought it meant.

She didn't want to hurt Mr. Big, but she knew she couldn't encourage him. No matter how loudly *if only* beckoned her heart.

"Were you able to get in?"

Bryce laughed a cocky laugh. "Let me show you."

For hours, they looked at the cases together. All three within a two-week period. Police had only recently begun looking for a connection.

The first case, they found out that the murdered man, a prominent professor at the University of Tennessee, had once been the professor for the first suicide victim.

There were strings of emails between the two from a decade ago. The emails they read through were mostly one sided. Professor Alleman verbally abused Jennifer Watkins, while promising he could help her if she performed sexual acts in return.

She skimmed the emails. Each one seemed more sickening than the previous ones. The messages stopped. Until recently. The victim turned the table and began threatening the professor.

A student found Professor Alleman with a letter opener jammed in his ear canal.

When the detectives combed through his emails, they went by Jennifer Watkins' home to find she'd taken an entire bottle of sleeping pills.

The coroner's report stated she was only thirty-two, but looked to be closer to eighty-two.

Police had no evidence linking Ms. Watkins to the professor's murder, but they believed she'd killed him.

Murdered victim number two, Mrs. Yolissa Holmes, electrocuted in her swimming pool. With no sign of the device that killed her in the water, the police determined she'd been murdered.

The lead suspect, Pam Jones, had a public altercation with Mrs. Holmes. Mrs. Jones had been having an affair with Yolissa's husband.

When the police went to question Pam, they found her dead, too. She'd slit her wrists. Again, her birth certificate stated she was only twenty-eight, but she looked to be in her eighties. The details of the rapid aging had been left out of the media. They were keeping that information silent.

The most recent case, a mother and a daughter. Found together at their home. The mother's neck had been broken—cause unknown. The daughter hanged herself from the balcony. Coroner found evidence of years of abuse on the daughter's body during the autopsy, leading them to believe the mother had been abusing her most of her life.

At only eighteen, Theresa Patton appeared in her eighties as well.

"I wouldn't have believed in witchcraft until I saw these reports," Bryce told her.

"Can you see if these are the first instances? Are there any similar cases outside of Knoxville?"

"What is the motive? Why do they look so old?"

"The suicide victims seek retribution for the pain they are in. The witch agrees to kill their nemesis for a price. She tricks them into *sharing* their beauty. Only they don't realize they've sold her *all* of their beauty. Once they realize what they've done, they can't live with themselves."

"How do you know this?" Mr. Big asked.

"I don't know. I just do. Like a puzzle, it all came together so clear in my mind."

"If the suicide victims offer to *share* their beauty for the murder of their enemy, what does it cost this witch to take *all* of their beauty?" Mr. Big made a valid point.

"That I don't know, but it can't be good."

"Why can't she just cast a spell to make her permanently beautiful?" Bryce asked.

"Evil witches are addicted to their power. They use it for all kinds of reasons. I've heard of many sacrificing their looks. Once a sacrifice is made, there is no undoing it. She can mask herself, but underneath, her beauty is all gone.

"If she only took a portion of the women's looks to commit the murder, it would cost her nothing to obtain the vengeance needed. Only her greed is ruling her, as she takes it all."

"I can do a search for others, but it's getting late. We have work in the morning," Bryce told her.

Kenzie stood. "What you've done tonight is a start. I can't thank you enough. Both of you."

Bryce nodded and left without taking his equipment.

Chapter 24

Colby

"How are you holding up?" Colby asked her. He didn't want to leave without knowing she'd be okay. He'd thrown a lot at her the night before, and now the weight of the more potential victims rested on her shoulders.

A storm brewed in those grey eyes of hers. A storm he would find a way to calm.

She huffed. "My Aunt Willow can look into the future. It's not exact. There are too many unknown variables, but she might be able to see who the next victim is. If I can find that out, I can find the Somes and stop her."

"How do you stop a witch?"

Kenzie looked away. A tear cascaded down her cheek. The urge to put his arms around her increased. He didn't know if, after last night, she'd push him away or welcome him.

Her silence worried him. "Kenzie, how will you stop her?"

"It's better you don't know," she whispered.

She hadn't admitted it in words, but he

knew. She'd have to kill the witch. Could Kenzie do it? She wasn't a killer.

He had to risk her rejection. Leaving her to face her responsibility alone was not an option he could live with.

He grabbed her hand in invitation. He wouldn't force himself on her. She turned and took the couple of steps needed before burying herself in his chest.

Colby considered offering to kill the witch for her. To live with the consequences of the murder of another human being instead of her having to live with it.

In his younger days, his temper got him into trouble. Trouble he could be in prison for. Only he'd been lucky. His temper had mellowed with age. Even in a drunken rage, he'd never considered killing anyone.

Kenzie had been groomed for this mission. She knew she might one day face an evil witch and bring about her demise.

What kind of man did that make him if he stood back and allowed the woman who held his heart to carry the full burden? Even if she never returned his affections.

She clung to him tight. Her lack of sobs increased his fears. Colby cupped her head and moved her to look at him. A numbness had overtaken her.

Again, he lifted her into his arms to place her in her bed, not knowing what else to do, as she appeared to have entered a state of shock.

He took her phone and held it up to her face to open it. Finding Remy's name in her messages, he sent him a message to come relieve him in the morning.

Remy may not want to fight the wicked witch of the west, but his friend needed him, whether he liked it or not.

Chapter 25

Kenzie

It had been a few days since she'd called her Aunt Willow and asked her to search for potential victims.

Bryce had found dozens of similar cases spread out across the country. Not one law enforcement division had connected any of them.

An hour into opening the bar for the night, she heard the disgusting sounds of mucus filled hacking, followed by the gasping sounds of desperation to find oxygen. Jamie.

She turned to find her yet again, upstairs, taking orders from a table. It still baffled her that Mr. Big managed to get his dick up for someone as grotesque as her.

Kenzie waited for her to pull out the nasty inhaler from her cleavage and use it to keep herself from dying from lack of oxygen before Kenzie yelled at her.

"Jamie, who'd you trick into switching with you this time?"

"What's the big deal?"

"Who?"

"Joan."

"Go back downstairs where you belong, and tell Joan to come see me."

"But..."

"Now, Jamie."

Kenzie watched the woman retreat. If she didn't need the help, she'd have fired her after the third time she found her upstairs.

She'd come to expect to find her blatantly disobeying her every shift. Why didn't she want the downstairs shift? Mr. Big. Jamie still shamelessly threw herself at him every night.

Jamie's screws were so loose, the woman believed he wanted her just as much as she wanted him. Kenzie overheard Jamie tell others on staff that him playing hard to get made them fuck like rabbits in heat when she got off work.

Kenzie knew better. He spent most of his nights with her in her apartment, reading over police files. Mr. Big had two, sometimes three, witnesses if he ever needed an alibi: her, Bryce and Remy. Jamie still referred to him as bae. Poor girl still couldn't tell anyone his name.

Kenzie didn't know it either, but by choice.

"Kenzie." Joan shrunk back as she approached her.

"Joan, what happened this time?"

"You know I can't say no to people. I'm sorry, Kenzie."

"Joan, you're going to have to figure out how

to. Jamie can't work up here. I shouldn't have to explain myself, but as long as she drinks on the job, she's better suited downstairs."

"I know. I know. I'm trying."

What did everyone see in Jamie? None of her staff seemed to be able to stand up to her.

She turned from Joan to see Mr. Big at the bar. When did he come in?

They hadn't spoken any more about making the most out of whatever time they had together. Not since she began the hunt for the Somes witch.

Kenzie made her way to the bar to take his order. He still insisted only she could wait on him, even though everyone knew what he would order. He had a regular choice for every night of the week.

"Sweetheart, can you do me a favor?" he asked as soon as she got close enough to hear him.

She crossed her arms, knowing him well enough to know this favor would send her eyes rolling back in her head.

"Can you smell me?"

"Smell you? You smell like an ashtray."

He smiled that smile. "Just smell me. I have this new cologne I'm trying out."

Remy bumped her hip. "Girl, if you don't smell him, I will."

She took a step closer and sniffed. Since her bout of Covid last Christmas, her sense of smell hadn't returned. She had to be nearly on top of something to smell anything. "I'm sorry. I can't smell very well."

"I need to know if it's any good. Try again."

She moved until her waist was flush with the counter. Sniff. Nothing. "I'll need to get closer if I'm going to smell anything."

She moved up on her toes to get closer as he leaned over the counter until his neck almost brushed her nose. She inhaled. The heavenly scent triggered a tiny flutter inside of her belly. *What the hell?*

"It's not too strong, is it? Just a hint of flavor. I'm going for sweet and desirable."

Another flutter. Like a butterfly struggling to take its first flight. She nodded her head in answer to his question while she backed away. Smelling something other than stale cigarettes and beer on his skin awakened something impossible to awaken.

She stumbled backward, away from the bar, and through the swinging door to the kitchen.

Remy followed her. "What's the matter?"

"My stomach fluttered." Her eyes bugged out of her head in confusion.

"What do you mean, your stomach fluttered?"

"I don't know. With my nose pressed in his neck, for a second, I felt something."

She wanted to smack the grin off of Remy's face.

"It's not possible."

"With true love, anything is possible."

"That's not how my magic works."

"You never did tell me exactly what words you used in your offering. Maybe there is something there."

"I don't know. Something like, I offer any arousal toward men who are just going to leave me in the end."

Remy's face looked as if it might split from the I-told-you-so grin stretched across his cheeks.

"What?"

"Don't you see, Kenzie, you didn't offer *all* of your hormones? Just the ones for men who won't last. He's your one."

"Impossible. The curse hasn't been broken."

"Something tells me it's coming. I have a feeling."

"You can't know that. None of us can."

"Fine, maybe it's a onetime fluke." Remy turned to the TV with the surveillance footage of the building. "I'm telling you, we have a ghost. Look, the motion sensor is going off and there's no one in the storage room."

Remy always had to have the last word when he believed something. Damn him and his damn ghost. And damn him and his damn ideas about true love.

Aunt Willow had finally seen something. She apologized for the delay. Said they were dealing with their own Somes' problem, but didn't

give her any details.

Angelina and Ana Adams.

Bryce did a background search on the women to save Kenzie from having to scry for them. One lived in Knoxville, and the other lived in Nashville.

Bryce even hacked into their phones after downloading a location finder app on her phone. She could see where both women were at all times. Whenever one moved toward the other, she'd get a notification. Hopefully, Angelina planned to leave Nashville to come after Ana in Knoxville instead of the other way around. She had a better chance of stopping them the closer she was to them.

Kenzie hadn't felt another flutter since smelling Mr. Big's neck. Thus, she brushed the occurrence off to a fluke. Remy didn't know what he was talking about.

She sent Leigh a text message about the witch not long after gravity released her from the episode she experienced. Kenzie had no idea if Leigh had the same number, but she had to try. She really could use her sister's help whenever she found her.

It had been a couple of weeks since the last murder-suicide. How the witch found her victims or how often she needed one baffled her.

Just as she made the last call announcement, a young man approached with a song request. He wanted to propose to his date, and apparently only worked up the nerve to go through with his plan at closing time.

She took the slip of paper with the song written on it to the piano. Kenzie read the title on the note. Another flutter. This time with two wings flapping.

Her eyes went straight to Mr. Big's. She hadn't meant to look at him, but once their eyes locked and she began to sing, she couldn't look away from him.

Before the third stanza, Mr. Big had made his way toward the piano. He straddled the bench and turned her head to meet his gaze. More flutters as he turned the song into a duet.

"I know you haven't made your mind up yet
But I will never do you wrong
I've known it from the moment that we met
No doubt in my mind where you belong"

He knew every word as they sang like two lovers in tune with one another.

She didn't pay attention to the young couple getting engaged. Her eyes never left the man singing with her, "To Make You Feel My Love."

She was so caught up in the moment and the nonstop flurries filling her belly, she hadn't noticed she felt rejuvenated instead of drained.

Their voices belonged together. Their souls melded. But how?

Mr. Big gave her his smile before leaning in and brushing his lips across hers.

Just a brush. Nothing more, but the power behind it. What the hell? How?

"What's your name?" suddenly she had to know. Her reason for not knowing it before—a memory.

He smiled and brushed the hair from her eyes. "Colby. Colby Parrish."

Chapter 26

Colby

Colby didn't even know he could carry a tune. His soul pulled at him when she began to sing Bob Dylan's song. So what if he knew who wrote the song and not just who sang it? He liked music.

The words came out as if he'd truly been bewitched. He didn't even try to fight it. Everything about the moment felt like destiny.

Fear kept him planted in the seat. The look in her eyes, the way she licked her lips after his brushed hers begged him to kiss her deeper —harder. Knowing all he knew about her, did he dare?

She answered the question for him when she closed her eyes and leaned in closer.

"Am I interrupting?" A woman's voice shattered the trance they'd both fallen under.

Son of a bitch.

"Leigh." Kenzie mouthed the woman's name before turning to look at her.

Her sister. What were the chances? Colby

put on a smile as he watched the woman driving him mad walk away.

"Are you really here?"

"I'd never let you face a Somes witch alone." Leigh stood a couple inches shorter than Kenzie. Same brunette hair, same stormy eyes. She had a tattoo sleeve on one arm while the opposite arm remained a blank canvas.

The tank top and jean shorts she wore put a picture of Kenzie in a similar outfit in his frontal lobe. Just what he needed, a new image to appear in his dreams.

Kenzie balled her fist and punched her sister square in the shoulder. He should've seen that coming, but he didn't.

"Where the hell have you been? Why did you cut me off?"

Leigh rubbed her shoulder. "We're doing this now? In front of him?"

Kenzie punched her again on the other shoulder. "I'll do this in front of whoever the hell I feel like doing it in front of."

Colby smirked. His woman could have turned and asked him to leave, but she didn't. Still, he respected her too much to gawk out of curiosity.

To keep from distracting her, he slipped out through the basement.

His only regret—not having her number to text her later to check on her.

He had no illusions about Leigh Wardwell's arrival. She made it clear she'd be another obstacle

he'd have to overcome on the path to Kenzie
Wardwell's heart.

Chapter 27

Kenzie

Kenzie pictured this moment in her mind thousands of times. Grabbing her sister, holding her tight and never letting her go. Only the second she heard her voice, all the pain she labored under because of her sister's abandonment took control of her emotions.

"I thought you'd be happier to see me." Leigh feigned innocence. No apology. No explanation.

"Happy to see you! After turning your back on me. I understood leaving our piece of shit mother in the dust, but me? What did I do to deserve your betrayal?"

Leigh looked unfazed. Her look Kenzie took like a slap to the face. How could she just walk in here like she'd done nothing wrong?

Anger bubbled under the surface of her control. Like a baby bird pecking at the eggshell it entered the world from.

Kenzie turned around. She wanted to see Colby's smile. His calming presence. Where did he go? His unexpected disappearance shattered a decade of control.

Every hurt, every bit of repressed pain pummeled through the deep recesses of each compartment she'd stored them in, in the form of a gut-wrenching scream through clenched teeth.

Suddendly, the hairs on the back of her neck stood on end. Colby.

Movement out of the corner of her eye made her turn. Colby stood on the top of the basement stairs. "You left me."

He ran to her. His hands cupped her hips as he tucked her in close. His head rested on hers. "I shouldn't have."

"You came back."

"I came back. I should have asked what you wanted. Do you want me to stay, or should I give you space to talk to your sister?"

Bats. Not butterflies. Bats. Damn wings were throwing a party inside her belly.

"I want you to stay, but you're right. I do need to talk to my sister—alone."

Colby stepped back. With his hand out, he demanded, "Give me your phone."

Kenzie opened her phone and handed it to him. He added his phone number and gave it back. He named himself "Old Man."

She laughed and edited it to Colby "Mr. Big" Parrish.

"Why Mr. Big?"

"It's the one that stuck. Mr. Big from *Sex and*

the City."

"Never seen it, but I'll watch it with you if you let me."

"Okay," she whispered, breathless.

"Call me or text me later. No matter what time it is. Just to say you're all right."

She nodded her head. Colby's lips touched hers again. Just a graze, but enough to stir the damn bats to life again.

She watched him walk away from her, not caring that her sister stood waiting for her and had witnessed the entire exchange.

"I can't believe you're being so stupid." Leigh had the nerve to tell her.

Kenzie turned and glared at her sister. "You lost any right to butt into my business."

She didn't drink often, but she needed one tonight. Maybe several.

"Really, are you a drunk, too?" Leigh asked her while she poured herself a shot of whiskey. Kenzie looked Leigh in the eye, her anger only growing deeper as she threw back the hot liquid.

"Like I said, you lost the right to butt into my business."

"Whatever. If you want to go down the same path as Mom, what's it to me?"

Kenzie poured another and another. The amber substance burned her throat, but she didn't care. She needed to feel something other than the feelings her sister's reunion stirred.

"Did you come here to tell me how to live

my life or to help me kill a witch?

"Don't answer that. Where have you been? What have you been up to? Let's catch up, baby sister."

"I'm here to help you kill the witch. You did text me. I thought you wanted my help."

"Too little. Too late."

Kenzie had no idea when the staff and the last of her customers left the building. She looked around at the mess left behind. They all got smart and took off, probably after the wail she let out.

Remy appeared. His hand rested on her back. "I locked up downstairs. I'll come back early tomorrow to clean up."

Remy had no love left for her sister. He grew up with her too and felt the abandonment in his own way.

"Hi, Remy."

"You've got some nerve, Leigh, walking up in here like erasing us from your life hadn't affected us. You decided you were done with us years ago, and I'm fine with keeping it that way.

"Kenzie, I'll be back tomorrow. If you smother her with a pillow in your sleep, I'll help you bury the body." He kissed her forehead and walked away without another glance at Leigh.

Kenzie followed him and locked the door behind him. "I'm going to bed. If you're still here in the morning, I'll fill you in on what I know. You can have the couch if you need a place to sleep."

She didn't bother to look back to see if her

sister followed her.

Chapter 28

Colby

It didn't take long for his brain to point out to him that walking out on Kenzie would only validate all the fears she'd lived with most of her life. Especially being abandoned.

Her scream sliced through his emotions. Ones he forced himself to keep in check. Going off on her long-lost sister wouldn't earn him any brownie points.

It surprised him when he got a text from her not long after he lay in bed.

Kenzie: When you do want to binge watch sex and the city?

Colby: The first night you can take off

Kenzie: Tomorrow too soon?

Colby: Only if you let me cook for you

 Kenzie: It's a date

He waited a few minutes after the bubbles on his phone disappeared before setting his alarm and rolling over to attempt to get some sleep.

Now that he had her number saved on his

phone, his phone nagged at him all day to text her. Being too eager might not go over well, so he ignored the urge.

Gourmet chef he was not, but he could put together an edible meal. He picked up some green onion sausage, rice, onions, and bell peppers to make his version of a redneck stir fry.

He considered flowers, but thought they might be over the top. He settled on a bottle of wine instead. Knowing nothing about wine, he stared at the wine choices for nigh on fifteen minutes before he settled on a Sauvignon Blanc with the word *Cupcake* on the label. Was it cupcake flavored or the brand name? He had no clue, but it looked pretty.

Having never gone to a woman's house to binge watch anything, he stared at his limited wardrobe, perplexed. He didn't have anything nice. His date-worthy attire hung in his closet back in Georgia.

He settled on a plain navy V-neck t-shirt and his Lucky brand jeans. Like a typical guy, he only traveled with his work boots and a pair of crocs for around the house. Crocs didn't seem like the right footwear for a first date, so he settled on his boots after cleaning them up a bit.

Colby splashed on the cologne he asked her to smell the other night. It didn't go unnoticed that the moment affected her. He nearly stole a kiss before she moved away from his neck. If she'd delayed a second longer, he would have.

Out of self-preservation, he tossed a pair of his flannel lounge pants in with the groceries. Watching a show with the word *sex* in it while she curled up next to him would be brutally painful in his jeans. He hoped his honesty when he asked if she minded if he got comfortable wouldn't put him in the doghouse.

What about the sister? Had Kenzie told her to get lost, or would she be there too?

When had dating gotten so hard?

Chapter 29

Kenzie

Remy about passed out when she told him she wanted the night off. Neither could remember the last time she did anything for herself.

She caught Leigh up on the witch hunt. They remained distant and neutral all day. Kenzie insisted if she wanted to crash on her couch, she had to help out in the bar.

After Leigh's nonchalant attitude, it surprised her when her sister agreed without argument to wait tables.

Before sacrificing her hormones for Remy, she'd hooked up with the occasional guy, but never at her place. And those rarely took her out on a proper date.

Colby wasn't going to knock on her door, escort her to his car, and take her to a fancy restaurant like a typical first date. The spur of the moment plans they made were more like third or fourth date activities.

She hadn't felt any life in her lady bits, but the bats going crazy in her gut were enough to make her consider helping him out with a blow job, at least.

The more she thought about the notion, "it's better to have loved and lost than to have never loved at all," the more she wanted to take the risk.

He made her want to risk it all. For one night, one day, one month, or one year. Going through the motions and fearing what might happen had become her prison—a prison which she resolved to escape from.

She couldn't remember the last time an evening allowed her the opportunity to dress in anything other than her uniform t-shirt and jeans.

Not wanting to add torture to Colby's libido, she decided to allow herself to wear her favorite comfy clothes that were perfect for dinner at home, followed by binge watching her favorite show.

Kenzie answered Colby's knock in her light cotton joggers, her Magellan fluffy socks, a tank top, and her favorite chunky sweater.

Colby's eyes swept over her from head to toe. *Damn. It doesn't matter what I wear. I'm going to give him blue balls in anything I put on.*

Kenzie looked down at the ground, embarrassed over what she did to him. *Maybe this was a bad idea.*

Mr. Big had this endearing move where he bent his knees while jutting his hips forward as his smile stretched across his cheeks. He'd tilt his head sideways until he'd shrunk himself down to her size in order to make eye contact. She hadn't noticed until this moment that he made the move whenever she shied away from him.

She picked her head back up to meet his confident gaze. Without thinking, she smacked her lips against his. The sudden unexpected move made her jump back before he could deepen this kiss.

"I think I made the right decision in packing my lounge pants for later."

He stepped around her with an arm full of grocery bags and headed to her meager kitchen.

She didn't even think to mention she didn't have a stove until he began unpacking his items on the counter. "All I have is a microwave and a toaster oven," she admitted.

Colby pivoted the top half of his body around. "I've lived in hotels for nearly a decade. You'd be surprised what I can do with a microwave and a toaster oven."

"Can I help?"

"Beautiful, take a seat and let me wait on you for a change." He pulled the chair out from under her two top table. She stared at the back of him, lost for words. He came off as cocky and arrogant nearly ninety percent of the time, yet he was:

    ✓ Thoughtful
    ✓ Caring
    ✓ Observant

- ✓ Patient
- ✓ Tender
- ✓ A cook
- ✓ Too sexy for his own good

If she'd ever made a list of quality must-haves in a man, he checked off all the boxes she would have created.

"How did it go with your sister?" He pulled her from the rabbit hole she'd gotten herself lost in.

She frowned. "I don't want to talk about her tonight. Can we just—you know—focus on us?" *If there is an us?*

He paused the meal preparation, leaned down and stole another light kiss, causing all the hairs on her body to stand on end.

Kenzie jumped to her feet. "Excuse me, um, I need a moment."

The powerwalk to her bathroom only increased her heart rate. She clutched the white porcelain sink while staring at herself in the mirror. *What's happening to me?*

"Kenzie, are you okay?" Colby's comforting voice on the other side of the door gave her the push she needed to face him. *Do I tell him what's going on? Do I give him false hope?* She splashed some water on her face before opening the door to face a worried Mr. Big.

"I've been alone for so long. I don't know how to do this."

The back of his hand grazed her damp cheek.

"You're not the only one."

Chapter 30

Colby

Following her moods had Colby's head spinning. He opened the door to the sexiest picture he'd ever seen in his thirty-eight years. Clearly, she thought dressing frumpy would keep his dick limp. Didn't she know clothes could never hide her beauty?

Beauty that went deeper than her outward appearance.

He brushed off her nervous greeting after she *kissed* him by keeping himself busy with dinner.

The sorrow in her voice when she told him she didn't want to talk about her sister tugged the strings of his heart. Stomping down the stairs to the bar where her sister waited tables to tell her just what he thought of her wouldn't go over well with either Wardwell.

For a split second before she hurried out the room, he could have sworn her pupils dilated with arousal *for him*. He trusted that she hadn't made it up when she said she couldn't get aroused.

Relief flooded him when he didn't have to beg her to come out of the bathroom she hid in. Only now they sat in awkward silence, eating the simple meal he prepared.

"Tell me about this show we're going to watch." He thought getting her mind off of them might bring her back out of the shell she'd sunk into.

She smiled at him, but it didn't reach her eyes. "Well, Carrie Bradshaw writes a popular dating column in New York City. It's her and her three best friends. Each episode, they fumble their way through dating, sex, and relationships."

"And who is this Mr. Big?" Getting her to put her focus elsewhere proved the right move.

"He's a bachelor. Older than Carrie. Set in his ways. They have an on again, off again relationship because they both have commitment issues.

"It's really a girl's show."

Colby clutched his heart and feigned offense. "Are you saying *I* can't enjoy a show about four women dating and having sex in New York City?"

She laughed. This time, joy reached those damn stormy eyes of hers that reeled him in from the start.

Kenzie tried to help clean up the mess he made, but he shooed her away. "It's my mess. I'll clean it up." Looking around at her apartment, it seemed she might not know how to clean up after herself. Colby kept his place meticulously clean.

Her disregard for a tidy home normally would make him reconsider his affections.

He was so far gone, head over heels, that none of his usual hangups could make him leave. She might not have forever in mind, but Colby had it all mapped out the moment she agreed to the date. Maintaining the domestic parts of a home he could commit to if Kenzie would open herself to the possibility that a curse only had as much power as one gave it.

Kenzie reminded him to change into the flannel pajama pants he brought with him.

He found her with her legs tucked in on the sofa and her HBO app opened on her television, waiting for him.

Colby took a seat on the side next to her with less space. He grabbed her knees, pulled them out from under her, and draped them across his thighs.

All she had to do was say the word, and he'd stay by her side until death. No curse would keep him from the best thing to ever happen to him.

Kenzie kissed his cheek before pushing play on the show he expected to only tolerate for her sake. He'd pay any toll required to spend time alone in her presence.

Six hours and one season later, Colby carried a passed-out Kenzie to her bed. He told himself he'd stay beside her until her sister showed up for the couch. He assumed it was where she'd sleep while in town.

He fell asleep holding Kenzie while listening for Leigh, who never showed.

Chapter 31

Kenzie

A body in her bed next to her startled her, as the sun beat down through her window demanding she start her day.

Cautiously, she rolled over to see if her sister or Colby had climbed into bed with her.

Colby lay on his back, shirtless, with a tent pole in his pants. Kenzie glanced over at her couch to see if Leigh had come upstairs during the night.

Not seeing her, she licked her lips and decided to go for it. *How hard can it be?*

She moved as slowly as possible to keep from waking him just yet. Getting up on her knees, she eased her hands into the waist of his boxers and sleep pants.

Not until his penis popped out from the band did he open his eyes. His hands grabbed both her hands before she could touch him.

"Kenzie, you don't have to." His just-woke morning voice came out raspy.

"I want to. Please."

With hesitance he released her wrists. He

hissed and thrust upward the moment her left hand cupped his balls while her right hand stroked his long, thick flesh.

"I've never done this before." He again grabbed the hand, stroking his shaft.

"Kenzie, are you a virgin?"

Too embarrassed to look at him, she admitted, "No, but I've never done *this*." Her mouth wrapped around his cock, already leaking precum. Slowly, she took him in inch by inch, careful not to graze his skin with her teeth.

The hisses of pleasure coming from Colby's lips gave her the courage to keep going. *If only* she could do more and experience all of him.

Would he hiss and hum while pounding her? Would he take her soft and slow at first and then go wild as she begged him for more? *If only.*

Despite the bravery coursing through her to bring Colby to completion, she couldn't bring herself to look at him. Had he closed his eyes? Or did he leave them open to watch her?

As he got nearer to his orgasm, he grabbed the sides of her head. Her hair tangled around his fingers while he held on and thrust in and out of her mouth. Through gritted teeth, he asked her, "Do you want me to pull out?"

She grabbed his hands and held them in place. She had no intention of giving him better than her all. Not after learning that even though guys came all over her stomach when they pulled out, many times they missed the pleasure of the orgasm because of the abrupt disruption in rhythm. She wanted Colby's legs to tremble. To know that she brought him to oblivion. That no other woman had the power to turn him into mush. Past or future.

He said her name as he came down her throat, followed by incomprehensible syllables. His hands fell from her head and his body lay limp.

She sat up to admire the picture of him spread out, sweating and sated before her.

Colby leaned up on his elbow and laced his hand back through her hair. "May I kiss you, Kenzie? A real kiss? One that expresses what you do to my heart?"

Chapter 32

Colby

Kenzie nodded her permission. She tried to stifle the look of pride in her eyes over what she did to him, but it was unmistakable.

In his encounters with women, whether one-night stands or the few relationships that failed, not one *ever* took all of him as she had.

She allowed him to mark her, to plant himself inside of her.

He sat up the rest of the way. With her consent, their lips met. Both of his hands went back into her morning hair. He took his time teasing her lips at first. She leaned in closer to him, stirring the passion inside of him. He knew then that he loved her. He loved her with an all-consuming need to be the one that defied any curse.

Her lips parted, inviting him to explore, to taste his essence on her tongue.

They hadn't joined their bodies as one, but the sensations flowing through his heart, his soul, screamed otherwise.

If they never consummated their love, he'd spend his life finding other ways to show her his love. She'd have to be the one to toss him on his ass—that was the only way any curse could separate them. Even then, he'd crawl on his knees through broken glass to get back to her.

She pulled away. Confusion replaced the earlier look in her eyes. Did he stir something inside of her despite her offering? Her look tempted him to ask, but he held back. If he was wrong, his assumption might push her away.

If he was right, she'd confide in him once she accepted his love and the happily ever after he wanted to give her.

"Spend the weekend with me?" He had the weekend off. His co-workers had gone home to Georgia to see their families.

Colby had his dog, but no other family he considered close. Just a few cousins. He was an only child and his parents had moved to Florida once they retired. The only one missing him in Georgia was his boy, Cowboy. Bryce promised to pick him up from the sitters for the weekend and spend time with him.

"I don't know if I can talk Leigh into working two more nights for me. I'm lucky she took one."

"I'm not going anywhere, Kenzie. If you have to work, I can sit at the bar or pour drinks with you."

Kenzie lay back on the bed and looked at the

ceiling. "What should we do?"

"I don't know." He lay down on his side after putting himself back in his pants. Staring at her, he couldn't fathom what he'd done right in this life. The honor of loving her should go to someone who didn't have a past filled with regrets.

"I've never been to Dollywood," he suggested.

"That would be a waste of money, since I'm terrified of rides."

"Ah, so no helicopter ride through the mountains, then?"

"I don't mind heights. It's falling from heights I can't stand."

"Heights come with the job for me."

"You never told me what you do for a living."

"You never asked," he teased.

She rolled over to face him. "I'm asking now."

"I'm a steel fabricator."

"I've heard of the skill, but I don't know what they do."

"The company I work for fabricates steel for construction projects. Mostly tall structures. I work on melting steel and shaping it to get it ready to go into place to hold up buildings. Wood only extends so far and can't be used on skyscrapers and commercial buildings like it can on houses, so we have to fabricate steel to hold up the structures."

"Sounds complicated and over my head."

"I usually just tell people I'm a welder. It saves me having to explain the process."

"How long have you been fabricating steel?"

"More than a decade. It's good money. It's the traveling that sucks and never being able to stay in one place for long."

Kenzie sat up. Worry wrinkled her brow.

Colby joined her and turned her head to look at him. "I lease a condo in Georgia because our company is based out of Georgia. I have no ties there other than my pit bull. My parents live in Florida. I have no siblings. It's just a job. I can get a job welding permanently in Tennessee. I'm not married to my condo or the company I work for."

She looked confused. "You don't live in Sevierville?"

He shook his head. "We all stay at an Airbnb about a mile from here."

Kenzie tried to look away. He knew the fear of her family curse weighed heavily with his revelation. "Please look at me, Kenzie. Look in my eyes."

She hesitated. He waited patiently. When she finally turned back toward him, a tear slipped past her control. He grabbed her face and looked deep into her eyes. "I'm not going anywhere. I've basically been a nomad for more than a decade. No more. When we finish the job here, I'll find something else. I promise."

Another tear fell. "A promise is a prison," she whispered.

"Not to me. A life without you is the prison."

Colby pulled her lips back to his. Damn this woman. Damn her fears.

She kissed him back. He felt a hunger in her kiss. A hunger for him to fulfill his promises.

The clearing of a throat, interrupting their moment, sparked the urge to turn and punch something.

Chapter 33

Kenzie

Kenzie backed away from Colby, but didn't give her sister the respect of turning to face her. Inside, she screamed with pent up frustration that her sister interrupted a pivotal moment—*again*.

"What do you want, Leigh?"

"I closed the bar, and it's all set up for tonight. I stayed up reading over all the documents you gave me. If it's not too much trouble, I'd like to lie down on the couch and get some sleep."

Kenzie ignored her sister's request for the moment. "Can I shower and get ready at your place?"

Colby nodded. She couldn't resist kissing the smirk on his face.

"Give me a few minutes to collect my things," she told Colby loud enough for Leigh to hear.

Kenzie hurried to pack a bag. She tossed in enough clothes for the whole weekend. It surprised her when she finished to see Colby back in his jeans, t-shirt, and work boots. Where had he changed? He didn't come into the bathroom while she gathered her makeup and shower supplies.

Colby took her bag from her and stuffed his pajama pants inside.

Kenzie took his hand. "I'll be back on Monday," she shouted behind her to her sister without giving her a chance to object.

With the door to her apartment at her back, she paused and sighed. Doing something for herself felt liberating. Not asking her sister for a favor, but demanding, had her adrenaline in overdrive.

In this moment, all of her responsibilities felt insignificant. For just one weekend, she planned to live for herself. To hell with her mother's bar and to hell with the witch she still had no lead on.

She sent Remy a quick text before telling Colby, "Lead the way, Mr. Big."

"You know he's older than I am."

"Is he? It's hard to tell with the salt and pepper in your beard and your bald head."

"Ha, ha."

Kenzie followed him out of her building and locked the bar back up. He hadn't been kidding about the closeness of the place he and his coworkers stayed.

"We have the place to ourselves. Everyone went back to Georgia for the weekend."

Colby opened the front door of the cabin on the mountain, void of any curb appeal. She knew the beauty of the home would be in the back of the house, facing the mountains.

She walked into an open floor plan with a spacious living room, kitchen, and breakfast nook. It took her by surprise how much neater a place full of men looked than her small apartment.

"My room is upstairs."

She followed Colby up the stairs in the living room area. They passed a ping-pong table in a large sitting area upstairs before walking into his room on the far wall. Two twin beds sat opposite each other in the room he led her to.

"You're a neat freak," she let slip.

Colby set his hat near the others he had lined up on his side of the dresser. He rubbed the top of his head while asking, "Is that a problem?"

"My place must have made you sick to your stomach," she worried.

"A little. I already planned to clean it the next time you go to work behind the bar." He pulled her into his arms and kissed her nose.

"I have no intention of changing my habits," she said, more to test him than anything.

"I've always believed that when you fall in love with someone, you commit to love them the way they are at that moment. If you can't love them as they are with no expectation of change, you don't really love them."

Did he just use the L word three times? Did he love her already? Did she love him?

"We still haven't decided what to do today?"

She sighed. "I rarely get the opportunity to do nothing. We're in a cabin with a view." She stepped over to the window. "I bet there's a gorgeous porch with a swing and a hot tub. I noticed a fireplace downstairs we can cuddle next to after dinner. Can we stay in and do nothing?"

He smiled. "Sounds dreamy."

"I would like a shower first. And to brush my teeth."

He rubbed his head again. Why was he nervous?

"May I join you?"

Kenzie's eyes grew. He wanted to get wet and naked with her. Why?

"Just because we aren't having sex doesn't mean we can't hold each other without clothes. I want to care for you. Give you those seven hugs a day. Show you the comfort having constant affection can bring."

His words woke up the damn bats. If only Leigh hadn't returned a bitch, she'd ask her sister for advice. What did she make of her body's feelings despite the offering she made to save Remy?

Chapter 34

Colby

"Stay just like that." Colby insisted once Kenzie stripped bare for him.

He didn't touch her. Not yet. He wanted to memorize her. So beautiful.

"You should just take a picture," she teased.

He raised his eyebrows at her suggestion.

"Go ahead. You know you want to."

Colby hurried back to his room for his phone. She raised her arms above her head and posed for him. He snapped a quick picture and set his phone on the sink.

"Just the one?" She poked her lip out, leaned forward, and pressed her breasts together.

Shit. What would she be like *with* a libido? He grabbed his phone again and took another picture.

She turned sideways and lifted one leg up behind her, the heel barely grazed her perfectly round globe. Putting her finger over her mouth to hush him, she looked directly into the camera.

Kenzie put on a show, allowing him to snap

picture after picture.

She grabbed the phone from him after more than twenty poses. He probably had at least a hundred snaps to admire in his leisure.

"Now you have something to look at when I'm not around to relieve your balls."

Colby gulped.

She turned the water on and waited for it to warm up.

He stripped out of his clothes. When she climbed under the water, he froze. The water cascading down her perfect curves made him grab his dick and start pumping.

She looked over at him. Her eyes danced with seduction. Kenzie glanced at his actions, but didn't object. She grabbed her body wash, poured it in a stream on her sponge while watching his every move.

He pumped harder and faster, watching her rub the soapy loofa all over her milky skin. When she used her fingers not holding the sponge and tweaked her pink nipple, he exploded.

How she satisfied him without intercourse blew his mind.

Kenzie stepped aside to make room for him in the shower. He tried to grab her and pull her close. Her hand to his chest stopped him.

She wagged her finger and shook her head. The sponge—still covered in her body wash—she rubbed over every inch of his body in slow motion.

By the time she brought the soapy mesh to

his dick, it was hard again. With one hand, she stroked his penis while the other moved up and down with the loofa.

Their eyes locked as she kept moving. Stroking, pumping, up and down. The head of his dick grazed her belly the harder she pulled him closer.

He couldn't look away. He wanted her to understand the profound effect she had on his soul. Colby shoved down the urge to close his eyes as she milked him until his cum coated her belly.

"Fuck, Kenzie. Three in one morning. You're killing me." When he pulled her to his chest, she didn't resist.

He kissed her with all the love flowing from his heart. Neither had admitted it, but he felt her love for him in that kiss. In the way her body shivered while he stroked her hips.

He wouldn't touch her. Not her pussy, not her breasts, not even her ass. Not unless she gave him permission. And he had no plans of asking her either. As they kissed, his certainty that he woke something in her she thought impossible deepened.

Chapter 35

Kenzie

What had come over her? She let him take pictures. The damn bats were out of control while he jerked off, watching her.

His body pressed against hers, his hands gliding along her slippery skin made her tremble.

No sparks ignited in her loins, but she started to believe Remy might have been correct. Maybe she hadn't sacrificed all of her libido. The words used in a spell were of utmost importance. It took careful planning, or one risked losing more than they intended to.

When she cast the spell to shrink Remy's cancer, she'd been in a dark place. An angry place. Bitterness filled the spell and the sacrifice. Bitterness that she hadn't the power to eliminate the cancer completely. A witch's life was the only thing of sufficient value to heal someone completely.

She allowed all of her pain over her mother, over Leigh's abandonment, over Remy's death sentence, over the curse, to spill forth into the words she chose to save him and into her offering.

Could the hurt she tapped into have unwittingly given her an out from her sacrifice?

She watched Colby make them breakfast in his boxers while she sipped on her coffee in her tank top and underwear.

Alexa played music in the background. She loved music. The power behind any song, especially written by the singer, she felt even when she didn't sing it.

A song could change her mood for good or for bad. It still marveled her that Colby's voice mixed with hers gave her energy instead of sucking it out of her.

Colby's hips swayed as "I Feel Good" by James Brown blared over the Bluetooth speakers in the kitchen.

He turned around with the spatula he used for the eggs. With his pretend microphone, he belted out the words. His voice—louder than James Brown's.

Kenzie laughed as he danced side to side with his spatula up to his mouth.

"God, I love you" slipped from her lips.

Shocked, she covered her mouth. He stopped in mid sway.

He fell to his knees in front of her. "You know I love you, too."

"I'm scared."

"I'm not. I have enough courage for the both of us."

She didn't want to dwell on the revelation any longer. "Is breakfast ready?"

He smiled in understanding. She kissed his beauty mole right under his eye.

Colby stood up and served them both a plate of fried eggs, sausage, and toast.

Chapter 36

Colby

He'd never had a more perfect day. Kenzie loved him. She admitted it. Now to convince her that he'd never willingly leave.

They watched some more of *Sex and the City.* He met Aiden and agreed with Kenzie. Mr. Big gave Carrie the freedom to be herself, but Aiden required too many compromises.

He did *okay* in the kitchen, but he mastered the art of grilling. They sat on the back porch overlooking the Smokey Mountains while he grilled sirloins and corn on the cob.

She opened up more about her childhood. How Leigh was before she went away. Life after her mom's arrest.

He told her about his childhood. His parents had him late in life. His mom actually believed she had stomach cancer when she first went to the doctor with nausea. They had been told they couldn't have kids. She fainted when the doctor announced to her at forty-five that she was pregnant.

They were beside themselves. He was the fulfillment of all their hopes and dreams. They spoiled him.

He couldn't keep a job because he knew his parents wouldn't let him fail. Until they retired and moved away, he hadn't had to grow up.

He drank too much. Got in too many fights. Put a few men in the hospital. His dad's pull as a police officer enabled him to escape punishment every time.

They moved for his own good, they told him. They'd had enough. With no one to turn to for money or to keep him out of jail, he got the wake up call he needed.

He got his shit together, but never found anyone he, for one second, considered worth making a lifelong commitment to.

Until Kenzie.

The beautiful fall night grew cold. Kenzie stripped naked again in front of him to climb into the hot tub on the porch after dinner.

Her pink polished toes wiggled at him from the water in invitation. Colby tossed his clothes on top of hers to join her.

The way she looked at him, he could have sworn lust lurked behind her eyes, and the way she shivered every time he touched her skin. Something nagged him to the point he felt pressed to question her more.

She settled into his chest. His dick rested against her backside. He rolled his eyes, imagining the feel of her sitting on him. His arms laced around her and pulled her into him tighter.

"Kenzie." He kissed the back of her neck. Her light hum gave him the courage he needed.

"Tell me more about how casting a spell works."

"Hmm, what do you want to know?"

"How do you do it? What do you do? How do you make the offering? All of it. I want to know."

"It depends on the spell. If it's a common spell, the ingredients needed, and the words to say, are written in one of our journals. Those who've used the spell previously even record what they sacrificed.

"For ones there's no record of, we have to write the spell. We find a quiet place while meditating on the situation and what we desire the outcome to be. The right words to a spell are critical. One wrong word and the whole thing could fail. Somehow, while meditating, the words just come. They fill my mind and my soul. I just know what to say.

"Ingredients aren't always needed. The burning of incense or a candle is sufficient for easy spells. For Remy—it's gross—but since he had colon cancer, he had to give me a stool sample."

Colby interrupted. "What about the offering to save him? How did you make it?"

"It's part of the words I said when I cast the spell. They came to me while meditating, too."

"Can I ask what those words were?"

"Why do you want to know?"

"Curiosity, I guess." He kissed her neck again.

"I'd have to check my journal for the exact wording, but it went something like, I offer any arousal for men who are going to leave me in the end."

Colby mulled over her words. Did that mean if a man existed who wouldn't leave her, she could feel arousal for that man? For him.

His resolve to convince her he'd never leave increased. Maybe she needed to believe it for her libido to surrender to him.

He'd considered a marriage proposal, but he didn't feel even *that* would convince her. Only time would, and getting to know the kind of man he was.

Colby held his woman until their bodies pruned. They had to hurry inside for towels, the cold bitter against their wet, naked bodies.

Chapter 37

Kenzie

Kenzie woke with the sunrise next to Colby in the beds they'd pushed together.

His query concerning her offering and Remy's indication that a man might exist who could awaken her libido annoyingly prodded her vexations.

Could Remy be right? If he was, why did she only feel hints of something and not full-blown passion?

If only she had the answer.

She grabbed her phone she hadn't bothered to check since texting Remy she'd be away all weekend.

Remy: Have fun. I got this.

Remy: Jamie didn't show 2 nights in a row. I still got this.

Remy: I might kill Leigh. I still got it. You better be having fun.

She put her phone back on the end table. Colby's soft snores made her want to leave him sleeping.

Kenzie crept downstairs for her morning coffee. She hadn't thought to bring her creamer, so she made do with the half and half in the fridge.

Being on the back porch, staring at the breathtaking view with her coffee and thoughts seemed like the way she should start every morning.

She could afford her own place like this, away from the bar. She imagined house shopping with Colby. At the same time, she heard Leigh calling her a fool.

In two weeks, her mom's parole hearing would take place. She still hadn't decided to attend. Leigh made a snarky comment, suggesting they were obligated to speak up for her. Let Leigh do it if she felt they owed their mother something.

Colby stepped out onto the porch with his own cup of coffee.

"Morning, beautiful."

"Morning, Mr. Big." Suddenly, she wanted to lick every inch of his body. Even though he wore long sleeves, pants, and socks to keep warm.

"You could have woken me."

"I like my mornings to myself with my thoughts."

"What kind of thoughts?" He sat down next to her. His leg pressed up against hers.

"I don't know. Like this morning, I'm realizing how much I'm missing living above the bar. I could get used to a view like this every morning."

"What's stopping you?"

"That's the thing. I don't know."

"I bet there are some open houses on the market. Sundays are usually a big day for that."

Kenzie titled her head and contemplated. *Should I look? What would it hurt?*

"We can go for a drive and look around."

"Do you even have a car here?" She poked at him.

"Good point. Do you?"

"I have a truck. Cars don't last in the mountains."

"I'm going to make breakfast while you search on your phone for listings." He kissed her breathless before leaving her alone again with her thoughts.

I'm going to do it. It's just looking.

She opened her phone to search for anything available within a five-mile radius. Preferably close to the bar.

Chapter 38

Colby

A morning looking at houses hadn't been what he expected, but it thrilled him. First she confided in him about the sudden desire and then she included him in her search. Progress.

They looked at five houses not far from *The Witch's Brew.* The third one hit him like a ton of bricks. He walked through the front doors into the kitchen of his dreams. Suddenly, he envisioned himself cooking for a family. Two toddlers running in circles around the bar laughing while he chased after them. Kenzie giggling behind her coffee cup in the breakfast nook.

She hadn't said much about any of the homes, but she took her time with each one. They were all furnished for the open houses, but she'd have to buy almost everything if she bought one. She had next to nothing in that apartment of hers.

On the drive back to his cabin, he asked her, "Did you see one you liked?"

She turned and grinned at him from behind the wheel of her 4x4 Toyota Tundra. "I put a bid in for the one with the island in the kitchen."

"When did you do that? We were together the whole time."

"I did it on my phone while you used the bathroom at the last house. I bid a little high and offered cash, so I'm hopeful they will accept my offer."

Colby choked on the word *cash*.

"I would have never guessed the bar brought in that much revenue."

"Not directly. My mother created a lucky potion I still sell to select clientele. It's not cheap, so it's made me very comfortable."

He raised his eyebrow. "Lucky potion?"

"As long as we don't use our powers for evil, we are allowed to earn a living with them. I don't know who originally sought my mother's services, but when she formulated the lucky brew, she made it endless. I sort of inherited it."

"Do you have a friends and family special?"

Kenzie looked out the window. Her voice, solemn as she answered his question. "Luck isn't always a good thing. Just because someone gets everything they *think* they need, it doesn't always lead to peace or happiness."

Colby reached over the console and squeezed her hand.

Her phone rang before either could say anything more on the subject.

"Can you answer it for me? Put it on speaker." She didn't recognize the number.

"Is this Ms. Wardwell?"

"Yes, yes, it is."

"This is Becky Sloane with Honors Real Estate. You put in an offer a couple hours ago for the cabin on Breezy Ridge Dr.?"

"Yes."

"The owners are moving out of state for work, and need to sell right away. Your cash offer has made their goals attainable. If you can wire a deposit today to the address in the email I'm sending, we can go to closing by the end of the week."

The end of the week. So soon. "I can do that. I'm driving right now, but as soon as I get home, I'll take care of it. Thank you, Mrs. Sloane."

"Thank you, Ms. Wardwell. You have made this couple feel very lucky today."

Colby set the phone back on the dash. She glanced over at him. He gave her a smile combined with a wink.

"How should we celebrate?" he asked her.

"Am I boring? I just want another night watching the sunset over the mountains while in your arms in that hot tub."

Colby grabbed her hand. "You're not boring. You're perfect."

Chapter 39

Kenzie

She hadn't run into Leigh since returning to the bar. Kenzie dreaded the lecture she knew her sister had rehearsed since she left with Colby for the weekend.

"Tell me everything." Remy cornered her while she loaded bowls with nuts and pretzels in preparation for the night.

Kenzie rolled her eyes. "I'm not telling you *everything.*"

"You better tell me something. If it wasn't for me, you'd still have your head up your ass."

"Really? You're taking credit for my happiness?"

"You know it's true."

Kenzie told him about Colby's insistence that they live in the moment. Make memories. Don't fear the future. If and when they parted ways, they'd have an epic story to tell. Even if they broke each other's hearts.

"Oh no. We are not losing him."

"We?"

"Yes, we. I won't have to worry about you here every night, all alone."

"I bought a house."

"What! When?"

"I put the deposit down yesterday. Closing is on Friday."

"I'm planning the housewarming party. We'll close the bar for one night—you can afford it. Start your wish list and send it to me."

Remy pulled out his phone and started making his own list. Kenzie knew better than to argue with him. Once he got an idea in his head, there was no changing it.

Leigh made an appearance not long after the bar opened.

"How was your weekend?" Leigh asked with contempt in her voice.

"Please tell me, what have I ever done to you to deserve the vile way you speak to me?"

Leigh bowed, "Forgive me, your highness." Kenzie didn't recognize the individual who had returned home with her sister's physical features who spoke with her sister's voice.

Her sister meandered around the room, checking on patrons. Kenzie needed the help with the bar and the witch—otherwise she'd tell her sister to go back to whatever hell spawned the new version of her.

Colby's body dip and smile rescued her from the putrid feelings festering inside of her over Leigh.

She stepped right into his open arms. "What's the matter, baby?"

How did he do that? He already read her moods like an open book.

They hadn't touched the subject of her sister all weekend. Part of being in a relationship meant opening up to the other person. Why did the thought of baring her feelings about Leigh seem more tortuous than being tied to a whipping post while she took lashes to her back?

"It's my sister. Soon, I'll tell you all about it." She lifted on her toes and stole a kiss.

"Are you walking out—again—on your responsibilities?" Kenzie wished Leigh had never come home. It hurt less not knowing what had happened to her.

With fire in her eyes, she approached her sister. "Bitch Leigh is not welcome here. If you can't find it in you to release the person who I grew up with—there's the door." Her finger shook as she pointed at the front door with the stained-glass window of a witch's hat.

> "Heart beats fast
> Colors and promises
> How to be brave?
> How can I love when I'm afraid to fall?
> But watching you stand alone
> All of my doubt suddenly goes away somehow"

Kenzie would know the voice filling the room from the karaoke machine anywhere, the one coming to her rescue. It might already be too late. She'd lost her temper and said exactly what she wanted to say.

She pried her eyes and emotions away from her sister toward the man displaying his heart for all to see. Including his co-workers sitting in their usual booth.

No one ever sang for her. Since Colby had entered her life, the number of tears she had shed was becoming absurd. She despised weepy females.

She mouthed the final words while Colby looked straight into her soul:

"And all along I believed I would find you
Time has brought your heart to me
I have loved you for a thousand years
I'll love you for a thousand more"

Colby's co-workers gave him a standing ovation. Hooting and hollering, yelling, "Encore! Encore!"

Colby held the microphone up to his lips. "Do y'all really want this old man to sing another one?"

The rest of the bar joined in the contagious ruckus from Colby's friends.

He winked at her. "I'll sing another song, if Kenzie will join me."

Whistles and cheers from her paying guests pushed her to the stage. Colby handed her the other microphone.

"Any requests?" he asked the audience.

It *would* be Remy making the suggestion.

Him and his meddling. "Tim and Faith's 'I Need You.'"

Colby wiggled his eyebrows and smiled.

Might as well do this right. She hopped off the stage, grabbed the closest chair, and handed it to Colby before getting another one. If Remy wanted them to perform the most sensual song country's favorite couple sang, she'd give the performance of a lifetime.

They took a seat across from each other. Colby bent over and grabbed the legs of her chair to pull her closer until they sat knee to knee.

The way the crowd cheered, one would have thought they were about to dance around a pole and strip for them. Or that they were the real Tim and Faith.

The lyrics showed up on the screen as the music started. Colby didn't bother looking at them as his eyes captured hers.

"I wanna drink that shot of whiskey
I wanna smoke that cigarette…"

Damn bats came to life as soon as the words to one of her favorite songs of all time came from the lips of the man she loved more than her next breath.

Her part nearly caught in her throat. The first couple of words were barely audible.

"… Lost in some corner booth, Cantina Mexico
I wanna dance to the static of an AM radio
I wanna wrap the moon around us, lay beside you

skin on skin

Make love till the sun comes up, till the sun goes down again"

If only reared its ugly head. What she wouldn't give to make love to him just once.

They joined their voices together for the last lines: "I need you."

The audience chanted, "Kiss! Kiss! Kiss!"

She wouldn't want to disappoint her fans. Kenzie stood up and moved her body in between Colby's open thighs. Cupping his face that never seemed to be without a smile, she brought her lips to his.

Probably more for the audience than for her sake, Colby's hands slid up the back of her thighs and landed on her cheeks. He gave them a squeeze.

The move made her giggle, thus breaking the passionate kiss.

Together they stood, laced their fingers, and took a bow.

Chapter 40

Colby

True to his word, a week after their weekend together, Colby snuck away while Kenzie poured drinks to clean and pack up her apartment. It didn't matter that she'd already signed the papers for her new place, and they'd slept there the last couple of nights.

He should have said goodbye because he had an early morning, but he wanted to stick around to let her vent about her sister.

He made his way back to the bar after making sure her place sparkled.

"Kenzie, I'm just not the same person I was ten years ago."

"Neither am I, but a decade didn't turn me into a monster."

Leigh closed her eyes. "The Kenzie I knew would never trust her heart to a man."

Colby cleared his throat. More to stop the two before they could cut each other any deeper than to make his presence known.

Leigh looked him up and down, making it

clear she'd never support their bond. "I'm going to bed."

He didn't bother watching the other Wardwell walk away. He only had eyes for his Wardwell.

"Do you want to have that talk now?" He brushed away the hair sticking to the corner of her eye.

"No, but I know I need to."

She accepted the hand he offered for him to escort her to a nearby table.

He patiently waited while she picked at the callous on his thumb.

Remy dropped off what looked like Long Island Iced Teas. Kenzie nodded her thanks at him and guzzled half of hers.

"My mom didn't always drink. At least I don't believe she did. I assume she loved my father. She never spoke to us about him. Not once. I don't even have a picture of him.

"I don't know how old I was when I noticed her slurring her words and tripping over her feet all the time.

"I'd wake up many mornings to find Leigh curled up in my bed because she was too scared to crawl into our mom's bed.

"We were close. We told each other everything. At least I thought we did.

"When she left, she left without a goodbye. At first, I swore she'd been kidnapped. Begged mom to call the police. Mom assured me Leigh left of her own free will and told me not to worry.

"Sister witches have a special bond. They can force comfort into the other with their touch—we call it comfort touch. It's more potent than regular human contact. We also are able to communicate telepathically.

"When Leigh left, she not only took the comfort only she could give me, she also severed our telepathic link.

"I've dreamed of her coming home and begging for forgiveness for so long. And now that she's here, I just want her to leave again."

She took the straw out of her drink and poured the rest down her throat. Colby slid his toward her. She needed it more than him.

The alarm on their phones went off at the same time. They grabbed them to check the app Bryce had installed. Colby insisted on having the notification signaling when Ana and Angelina Adams entered the same city.

Leigh came running at them with her phone in hand.

Angelina had just entered Knoxville. Kenzie rushed to find the keys to her truck. She raced out the door with her sister, leaving him behind.

He downed the rest of the Long Island Iced Tea Kenzie left behind. The glass shattered when he slammed it down too hard in frustration.

"They've been trained for this." Remy's attempt to ease his mind only pissed him off more. He accepted the towel and broom Remy handed him.

Cleaning helped calm him only slightly.

Remy carried a case of Coors to the table and joined him. "I'm not going anywhere either until I know they are safe."

Colby clicked the neck of his beer against Remy's. Screw waking up early. He wouldn't get a wink of sleep until Kenzie returned unharmed.

Chapter 41

Kenzie

Leigh navigated while Kenzie drove her truck like a race car through the winding roads.

Neither sister knew what to expect. How did the witch find her victims, or did they find her?

Kenzie didn't know if she wanted to find the witch with Angelina so she could kill her or find the sister alone so she could talk her out of whatever vengeance she had planned.

Ideally, finding Angelina with the Somes would end the chase sooner rather than later. If they weren't together, they would have to go back to Aunt Willow and ask her to search for more potential victims.

The app led them to a Rodeway Inn. Bryce's app had to have been government grade. As they jumped out of the truck, it led them right to Angelina's room.

Leigh banged on the door of Room 107. Fortunately, the doors were on the outside. If they had to take down a Somes in a hallway in the middle of a busy hotel, too many people could get hurt.

A petite woman close to their age opened the door. Leigh crossed her arms. "Didn't anyone warn you about opening the door to strangers?"

Leigh's attitude and posture put fear in Angelina as she tried to slam the door in their face. Leigh moved faster. The foot of her boot in the door kept the woman from closing it.

Leigh pushed her way into the motel room.

Kenzie surveyed the room while Leigh opened the bathroom and the closet. Empty.

"Where is she?" Spittle flew from Leigh's lips.

Angelina trembled. "Where is who?"

Kenzie grabbed her sister by the elbow. "A softer tactic might work better."

Leigh pulled her arm from her sister's grasp. "*Veritas,*" she commanded of Angelina.

Angelina fell to the bed, trembling. With a quivering lip, she admitted, "I came to find my sister. She has my child."

Kenzie sank to the floor and took Angelina's hands in hers. "Angelina." The woman's eyes bulged when Kenzie called her by her name.

"I don't know why your sister has your child. I can only imagine the pain you are suffering. Your pain is attracting someone evil. Someone who will give you the vengeance you seek while stealing your life in return. She will make pretty promises, but will only tell you half-truths.

"I'm Kenzie and that's my sister Leigh. I don't care for her very much right now either. She commanded the truth to come from you, but her command also means you'll recognize if we're telling the truth.

"You're not safe here. You either need to go home and forget whatever vengeful plan is running through your head, or you need to come with us. We can keep you safe. I can't promise you the evil one won't find you back in Nashville and persuade you to come back here."

"You need me to stop her, don't you?" Angelina asked.

Kenzie nodded. "We've been hunting her. She's killed six people in Knoxville and dozens more across the country. She murders the one causing the unforgiveable pain and what she does to the other is so horrible they commit suicide. If you let her kill your sister, the revenge will be sweet, but the consequence will cause you unimaginable pain—pain so great that you won't be able to live with yourself."

"How do you know all of this?" Angelina had calmed down since Kenzie took control of the situation while Leigh watched the parking lot from behind the curtain.

"We're light witches, and the one coming for you is a shadow witch. We know she's coming for you because we have a seer who saw her with you and your sister."

Angelina studied Kenzie. "I still don't

understand why I believe everything that you're telling me."

"You're under a truth spell. You can only tell the truth while also recognizing truth from fiction."

"Lie to me."

"Our mother is back at our bar waiting for us to bring you there," Kenzie told her.

Angelina sat back in awe. "I could feel the lie. It washed over me like a really bad feeling, only deeper."

Kenzie nodded.

"How long will it last?"

"We'd have to release you from the truth spell. It will only work between the three of us, as we were the ones together when my sister cast the spell."

Angelina bobbed her head in understanding.

"Can you help me get my child back?"

Kenzie nodded her head. "We'll listen to your story. We can't promise anything. All we can do is offer advice. If we are able to help, we will, but I don't want to give you false hope."

Chapter 42

Colby

"I'm—taller. I should—be—*hiccup*—Cher." Remy stumbled on to the stage.

True, if Colby had to guess, Remy towered over his six feet at six-fourish. "But my voisp is deepers."

Two grown drunk men arguing over who would sing Sonny and who would sing Cher. Only strangely neither wanted to play Sonny. One would imagine two grown men would fight over not getting stuck singing the woman's part.

"Okay, okay, fine, you be Sonny and I'll be Cher," Remy suggested.

"Okay. Goood idea."

Remy tapped his foot, waiting for his line to scroll across the screen.

"They say we're young and we don't know, we won't find out until we grow."
Drunk Colby didn't miss his queue.

"Well, I don't know if all that's true, 'cause you got me, and baby, I got you."
Together in harmony, they belted out the

chorus:

"Babe,
I got you, babe.
I got you, babe."

Remy tossed his arm around Colby, and they swayed in sync, not noticing the girls had returned.

Colby lifted his eyes in the direction of the girls, stopping mid-Babe. He tugged on Remy's shirt. "Remy, Kenzie's bap."

Hiccup. Remy raised both hands and his microphone in the air. "Kenzie. *Hiccup.* You're not —dea—dd."

Colby stumbled from the stage, nearly faceplanting on the floor to get to Kenzie.

His stood in front of her, blowing his beer breath in her face. "I love you."

Kenzie giggled.

Leigh hmphed. "Seriously, a drunk. Kenzie, he's probably only screwing you for the free beer."

"Leigh, that's enough. In the few months that I've known him, I've never seen him drunk."

"Yeah, and Kenzie can't have sex anypay." Colby whispered while falling halfway into a chair luckily positioned behind him. He grabbed Kenzie's hand and brought her fingers to his lips. "I love you."

He looked over at Leigh and pointed at her. "I don't lipe you." He swiveled to find Remy. "Remy, I luuv you." Colby noticed the petite, pocket-sized woman with them. "I don't know you."

Colby slid from the chair to the floor. He flapped his arms and legs, making pretend snow angels.

"Remy, I didn't know the beer was free. You owe me a refund."

Remy stumbled toward the front door.

"Where are you going?" Kenzie worried.

"Kelly is outside. *Hiccup.* I texted him—when I saw you weren't—deadd."

"Well, that's one less body we have to move tonight," Leigh sarcastically added.

"I'm not moving him. I'll grab a couple pillows and a blanket from upstairs. You and Angelina can flip a coin for the bed or the sofa."

Colby continued to make snow angels while Kenzie hurried upstairs.

He heard muffled arguing, but the fog in his brain kept him from making out the words. He just knew he didn't like whatever negative opinion Leigh tossed at his Kenzie.

"Leigh, leave Kenzie alone," he managed to call out before succumbing to the alcohol. His snores permeated the air.

Chapter 43

Kenzie

Her back ached from curling up next to Colby on the floor last night.

Bryce got her text message she sent him from Colby's phone and surprisingly managed to rouse Colby for work.

She imagined he spent the day hungover and exhausted. Only he meandered into the bar with his giddy grin.

He took a seat at the bar. "Did I say or do anything I shouldn't have last night?"

It embarrassed her that he mentioned her sex limitations, but she refused to hold it against him. Drunk people rarely had control over the words that vomited from their mouths.

Kenzie shrugged her shoulders with a bonus you'll-never-know wink.

"I'm sorry." Colby leaned over the counter and kissed her before heading to the table with his work friends.

For a Monday night, the bar surprisingly had filled up for dinner, keeping her too busy to spend any time with Colby.

Closer to closing time, Jamie sauntered through the front door, acting like she owned the world. She'd better not want her job back.

Leigh spit her water out. *"It's her."*

Her sister's voice back in her head made her stumble. *"Her who? That's Jamie. The no-show server."*

"That's the witch. The one we're looking for."

Jamie sashayed over to the table where Colby hung out with his co-workers. Surprisingly, without stumbling over from whatever her choice of liquor for the day might be.

"How do you know that?"

"You can't see what she wants you to see. Can you?"

Kenzie stared at her sister, perplexed. *"Kenzie, repeat after me. Oculi Videre."*

She might be pissed at her sister, but she trusted her. *"Oculi Videre."*

Like bad reception, Jamie's appearance flickered in and out in front of her eyes. The woman in thick glasses, with fat rolls, and stringy hair stood over Kenzie's man, looking like someone out of a Playboy magazine.

"Jamie Moses." Kenzie slapped her hand over her mouth at the realization. *"She transposed Somes. How did I not see it?"*

"She had a veil over her. Only you could see her

true self. While everyone else sees who she wants them to see."

"Why didn't the veil work on you?"

"Mother opened my eyes a long time ago." Leigh offered no other explanation. Why did their mom open Leigh's eyes and not Kenzie's? A question for another day.

"Why is she here? And why is she near my man?" Kenzie remembered Angelina upstairs. Oh no.

"We can't focus on that. You pull the fire alarm. I'll get the potion."

Kenzie followed her sister's instructions without delay. Staff and employees rushed out of the bar in a panic. The unexpected smoke coming from the kitchen added to the hysteria.

"It needs to be believable, or everyone will stand around and ask questions." Leigh told her while holding the potion to freeze Jamie in place in the palm of her hand.

Damn Colby ran to her side instead of out the door, worried for her. *"Colby, it's her. Get out of here."* She motioned her head toward the door, hoping he'd understand the hint.

His eyes bugged out of his head. He leaned down and whispered to her. "I'm not leaving you."

He heard me. How?

"What luck? You emptied the entire building for me. Well, except for this idiot." Jamie waved her hand up into a fist and spat, *"Er."*

Leigh tossed the potion to immobilize the witch at her feet.

Everything happened simultaneously. Jamie's spell, the potion at her feet, and Colby's body flying up into the air. He thrashed about, struggling. He hung suspended in the air as if he had an invisible rope around his neck. His hands desperately fought to grab hold of something to release its grip.

Kenzie watched her greatest fear unfold in front of her. She stood in shock. Why didn't she listen, knowing the curse would take him from her somehow?

Everything happened in slow motion.

Jamie cackled behind her. Leigh held a distinctive hunter's knife in her hand, ready to take out the witch.

"You think killing me will save him? It won't," Jamie heckled.

Kenzie could do nothing but watch the man she loved choke to death. The power to reverse another witch's spell didn't exist.

Remy burst through the front door. He looked around at the scene before shoving a barstool under Colby's feet.

He still struggled with the tight noose around his neck. Not one of them could remove it. Only Jamie could. She told the truth. Her death wouldn't void what she'd done.

Tears streamed down Kenzie's face as she helplessly watched Colby take his last breaths.

Searing fire took hold of her forearm. She bit back the scream forming in her throat. Pain like she'd never experienced burned under the surface of her skin.

She never took her eyes from Colby. No amount of suffering would make her look away. Strange. He'd grabbed his arm as if it burned as well.

Without warning, Colby's body fell to the floor.

Kenzie ignored the wailing powerful enough to shake the chandeliers as she ran to Colby's lifeless body.

"No, no. It can't be. It's not possible," Jamie ranted behind her.

Kenzie felt for his pulse. She couldn't find one. Frantically, she started CPR.

Remy yanked her from him. "Let me. You're too emotional."

She nodded. Rage bubbled up inside of her. Like a tornado of force, she turned toward the Somes, who still dared breathe in her presence.

"Give me the knife, Leigh!" she shouted.

Leigh sheathed it behind her back. "No, Kenzie. It's over. Her powers are gone. Our curse is broken. If we kill her, we become her."

Kenzie moved to fight her sister for the knife, not processing what her sister told her.

"It's over. We're free."

"You only think it's over. We'll get it back. We'll petition the father of shadows. He will bless us again."

Kenzie stopped fighting her sister for the knife and turned back toward Jamie.

"I may have failed with him for now, but my family will get his name and picture once I leave here. They'll come for him to finish what I couldn't. Just like they're coming for hers." She tossed her head in Leigh's direction.

"Her what?"

"Ask her. She felt it. She's marked too."

Kenzie lifted her arm where moments before it burned like she'd been branded. A perfect circle had been left behind.

She looked at Leigh, who held out the opposite forearm. Leigh had one too.

"My family has his picture and his name. They will come for him and any others. We will not stop until all of your other halves are killed or stolen. Preferably stolen—the pain is so much sweeter when they choose us over you."

"Who is she talking about? Leigh, do you have someone in your life?"

Leigh shook her head.

"What are these circles?" Leigh asked Jamie.

"My family put them on your family centuries ago, buried under the surface. Only we could see them. It's how I found him, and how I knew he'd lead me to you."

Chapter 44

Colby

Colby coughed. He wrestled for the invisible object keeping him from breathing. He violently cleared his airway amidst more coughing. His throat burned like acid.

Remy grabbed his shoulders and steadied him. "It's over. You're okay."

Colby sat up and looked around. Kenzie stood with her back to him.

"Who's the ugly broad they're talking to?" Colby choked out through the pain in his larynx.

"That's Jamie. The one who called you bae."

"What happened to her?"

"That's the real her."

"Shit. That's freaky." Colby had his hands on her. He fucked her, and she felt and looked like a beautiful woman. Not anymore.

Remy helped Colby stand. They moved closer to hear what the three of them talked about.

A mark. Colby remembered the feeling of being branded while he hung in the air. He knew the feeling because he'd voluntarily let someone brand his shoulder after a drunken night. He held his arm up. Inked over one of his ladies, he now had a perfect circle.

He moved closer. His arms snaked around Kenzie. He cared no more about what the witch had to say. She needed to know he lived.

Kenzie jumped and turned around to face him. Tears of pain were replaced with tears of joy. She reached up and touched his face. "You're still here. You're never leaving me."

He smiled and nodded. "I'm never leaving you."

They tuned out the rest of the world. The rest of the evil Jamie spewed. Obviously, she'd sacrificed her sanity to steal her victims' beauty.

Nothing and no one else mattered as they kissed the kiss of true love.

Kenzie shoved him away. The look of shock on her face told him everything he needed to know. She wanted him. Her belief that he'd never leave freed her libido.

Colby smiled. He moved to claim her. To show her how a man loves a woman with everything within him.

The asthmatic attack from the insane bitch behind them burst their bubble.

"It's in her cleavage," Kenzie told Leigh.

Leigh spoke the word, "*Dimittis*."

Jamie stumbled forward from the release. She again had full control to move about. She fumbled in her bra for her inhaler. Her lungs constricted further as she grappled to find it.

Colby felt nothing but disgust as she struggled to breathe.

Finally, she found her inhaler and pulled it out of her sweaty boobs. In a panic, she shook it with such force her unsteady fat feet flowing over her high heels twisted out from under her.

Jamie fell backwards, impaling her head on the leg of a chair that had been knocked over in the panic to exit the building after the fire alarm had gone off.

All the way through her skull to right between the eyes. Like something out of *Final Destination.* He wouldn't have believed it if he hadn't witnessed it.

Blood pooled under her head. Kenzie turned her head and buried it in his chest. She couldn't stand the sight of it.

How did he know that? He heard and felt her discomfort. Just like he'd heard her voice before telling him to "get out."

"I'll explain it all. I promise."

"I heard you again. I heard you before."

She bobbed her head in his chest. He wanted answers, but knew they had to deal with the body behind them first.

Chapter 45

Kenzie

In all the commotion, Angelina disappeared. Leigh went to look for her when they didn't find her upstairs. She had to have run out with the crowd when the fire alarm when off.

The fire burning in her loins for Colby hadn't waned. Not even as she watched the leg of a chair puncture Jamie's skull.

Colby's voice in her head only stoked the fire. No one had told her they'd be able to communicate telepathically with their soulmate once the curse broke. It made sense, though.

Who broke the curse? What happened? There were more Wardwells than she'd ever met, so chances were slim she'd ever know the full truth. She planned to call Aunt Willow the second things calmed down.

Leigh took charge and called the police. Kenzie pulled up the security feed for them. She started it from the moment Leigh released her. The authorities didn't need to see everything else that went down. They only needed to know Jamie hadn't been murdered.

Colby hadn't left her side. The giant grin on his face only made her lady bits throb every time she looked his way. They hadn't talked about it, but he knew.

She wiggled in her office chair. The need to get out of there and jump him wouldn't allow her to sit still.

It all still confused her. The circle on their arms. What Jamie said about her family placing it on them. Leigh's man. Who was he? The ending of the curse. Her libido. Colby's soul in her soul.

She hadn't dared open her soul to his all the way. She knew it would be full of all the things he planned to do to her the second they were alone.

If she heard even one, she might strip for him no matter who was around.

A volcano crested between her thighs. Lava pushed at the surface. Any minute she'd burst, and nothing would put back the rush, seeking what only Colby could give her.

They gave the police the footage. "Do you need me for anything else?" she practically begged them while Colby's fingers danced along her waistline.

"No ma'am. We have all we need."

The coroner had loaded Jamie into a body bag while she'd been in her office.

Leigh and Angelina sat in a corner booth in deep conversation. Kenzie trusted that with Jamie gone, Leigh could handle Angelina. The two had spent the whole day bonding, which surprised Kenzie and stung if she was honest with herself.

She didn't bother asking Leigh or Remy if they needed her when she grabbed Colby by the hand and pulled him out the door.

Kenzie tossed him the keys to her truck. Once inside, she leaned over the console. She couldn't wait another second to feel his hard appendage in her hand.

He looked at her out of the corner of his eye as he raced to her house. Their house. He didn't know it yet, but he wasn't going to lay his head anywhere else ever again.

She'd just signed the contract and only had a mattress tossed on the floor of the master bedroom. She hadn't even bothered to look at other furniture yet. Not with everything else going on.

The tires of her truck squealed as Colby pulled into the driveway.

She jumped out before he could open her door.

Colby kicked the front door shut with his foot. He spun her around and pinned her up against the pine. His fingers traced from her cheek, down her neck, along the side of her breast, until he stopped at her hip.

Her chest rose and fell, heady with unbridled desire.

"Kenzie, say you want this," he demanded.

She gave him more than just her yes. She closed her eyes and opened her soul wide.

Colby's hands fell to his sides, as every bit of her need for him flowed from her to him.

Chapter 46

Colby

He had no idea how Kenzie poured all of her thoughts, her feelings, her desires into him. He only knew he needed to reciprocate.

Colby closed his eyes and let his instincts guide him as his soul reached for hers.

If he died tonight pleasuring her, it would all be worth it.

When he opened his eyes, she was gone. He heard her laughter coming from the bedroom. Knowing she'd already stripped bare, he took everything off before going in search of her.

He'd rehearsed asking her what she wanted many times while he fantasized about being the one to arouse her. How did she want him to take her the first time? Now, with her desires inside of him, he already knew. He knew every imagining burning within her.

He found her just like he knew he would, spread out on the mattress. Her legs opened wide, her fingers rubbing her clit in invitation.

They hadn't discussed protection, and neither considered it amidst the fog of passion controlling their every move.

Colby lined himself with her entrance and thrust himself inside of her walls in one move.

Her body bucked up toward him. Her fists gripped the sheet underneath her. Her need so great she came the moment he pierced her.

He stilled while her tight pussy clamped hard around him. If he dared move, he'd come undone before he could enjoy the feeling of finally being inside of her.

She looked at him with bliss and patience. She felt desperate for him to pound her, but lay there with understanding as he calmed his dick.

Once his blood slowed enough for him to be ready, he gave her what she needed. She didn't have to beg him to fuck her harder or deeper, because he was in tune with just how deep and how hard she needed him.

"Colby, yes, Colby," she screamed out his name as she came undone again. For him. Because only *he* could pleasure her.

His body quivered and pulsed sooner than he wanted to. His legs trembled as he struggled to hold himself above her.

Kenzie looked like a goddess splayed out underneath him.

She jumped up the moment he rolled over

to lay beside her.

"Where are you going?" he called after her, out of breath.

"To clean up. When you recover, you're going to show me what you can do with that delicious tongue of yours."

Yep, he might need to go for a checkup. Make sure his ticker was up for the ride known as Kenzie Wardwell.

Chapter 47

Kenzie

Kenzie ran a bath in the whirlpool jacuzzi in the master bathroom. She slipped below the water, letting it wash over her.

With the momentary satisfaction, she needed space to process the overload of information and feelings that hit her all within the last couple of hours.

If she had her phone, she'd call Aunt Willow.

She grabbed her sponge and her body wash. Before she finished sudsing the loofa, Colby stood over her, holding out her phone.

"Thank you."

"Anytime, my love."

She liked being called his love. More than sweetheart, baby, beautiful, and all the other names he'd tried out on her.

Finding her aunt's number on her phone, she hit the green call button.

"Kenzie. You felt the curse break."

"I did. Did you?"

"I watched it break. My granddaughter succeeded."

She hadn't ever met Aunt Willow in person or her family.

"Can you tell me about it?" she asked her aunt.

An hour later, her aunt had told her everything.

Kenzie shared with her about Jamie and what she'd learned from her. Along with the threats she made toward her and Leigh's soulmates and how the rest of her family wouldn't give up.

She told her about Colby. Not about him being the only one to wake her libido, but about their connection. "We have the telepathic link."

"So do my granddaughters with their soulmates. We knew that Emma Wardwell upgraded the Turner family's soulmate call when she made it possible for them to pass the gift along to others. The caveat–we know about the call, so we've been able to tap into it, too."

"It's powerful, Aunt Willow. Not even close to my connection with Leigh. He's a part of me. I'm a part of him."

"You've earned it. We all have."

"It seems too good to be true."

"Possibly. We can guarantee the Somes will

retaliate. Whether the father of shadows wipes his hands of them is another matter. If not them, another family will accept the evil he offers, and it will be up to us to stop them."

"Thank you, Aunt Willow, for everything." Kenzie paused. "Have you talked to Mom?"

"She misses you."

"She's up for parole."

"She told me."

"I don't know what I'm going to do."

"Let your heart guide you. She won't lead you down the wrong path."

They said goodbye. Kenzie climbed out of the tub, ready for round two with her man— her soulmate. Something she believed she'd never have.

Colby, her soulmate, lying on his back with his hands behind his head, stirred every desire in her loins. At least the damn bats were hibernating, since the knowledge that her man would never leave her woke what she believed she'd never experience again.

She never asked him, but he must work out. His chest muscles flexed as she admired his clearly defined body.

A light flush spread over his cheeks as her eyes took him all in. "Like what you see, my love?"

Kenzie sucked in her lower lip. Her teeth nibbled on the plump flesh.

Colby jutted his taunt length into the air in invitation. Like a lioness on the prowl, she fell to her hands and knees. With stealth, she eased her body toward his throbbing member.

Before she could wrap her lips around what she craved, Colby jumped up and tossed her onto her back in his own stealthy move.

"You said you wanted to know what talents my tongue could perform. Or did you forget?" His fingers grazed the inside of her thigh. Her lips parted as she sucked in oxygen. Fire surged through her veins with just the touch of his calloused fingers.

Kenzie's knees fell open like paper in a cool breeze.

A grin spread across Colby's handsome face as he shook his head. "Did you think I was just going to dive straight into your pussy while neglecting the rest of your body?"

He reached for her foot. Gently, his hands worked through the aches in her arches from spending long hours on her feet.

"This candy red is my new favorite color." His lips grazed the tips of her toes before moving to her arch. First her left foot, followed by her right. His lips followed by swirls with his hot tongue covered every inch of her all the way up her body.

She hissed in anticipation as his tongue moved closer to her juices dripping onto the sheets. Kisses trailed along her inner thighs as her body screamed for him to keep moving.

His hot breath stoked the embers of her ready garden. His fingers spread her lips wide as she watched him admire the picture before him. His lips puckered. She stifled the urge to scream for him to get on with it, knowing he could hear her every desire and still teased her. He blew upon her entrance, only to skip her wet pussy. His tongue danced around her belly button.

She no longer stifled her desire to scream. She clamped the sides of his head with her thighs and pushed his head back toward her burning pussy.

Chapter 48

Colby

Colby chuckled at her impatience. The desire to drink of her burned just as deeply within him.

Having her in his head, hearing thoughts usually kept private, stirred up a primal need to keep her begging. Her desperation would have him soon standing over her, beating his chest shouting "MINE!"

Hungry for all of her, he spread her open wider as his tongue took liberty, starting with the back and licking upward in one full scoop.

An unintelligible roar escaped Kenzie's diaphragm as she bucked up against him, prompting him to repeat the same move several more times.

Her juices soaked his beard even before his tongue speared her entrance. Kenzie's fingers tried to sneak in to play with her clit. Only Colby pushed them away. *"Not yet,"* he whispered through their bond.

"Good girl," he praised when she obeyed.

Her thighs clamped around his head again as he tongue fucked her pussy.

"Please, may I cum?" echoed on repeat.

Colby pulled away. "Does my baby want to cum?"

She looked at him with wanton eyes and nodded vigorously.

With his thumb pressed against the star of her butthole, he rubbed circles. The two fingers on his other hand breached the entrance of her vagina. His other thumb pressed against her clit, moving back and forth and side to side.

"That's it, baby, cum for me," he ordered.

Her body writhed under his control, pulsing with the longest orgasm Colby ever felt a woman experience.

Kenzie's whole body went slack the second the waves receded.

He briefly watched the woman he loved more than his own life laying beneath him in contentment. "I'm not finished with you," he promised.

Her heavy head turned toward him. Through the slits of her eyes, she smiled up at him. "You better not be."

Colby planned to have his woman in every position before they went back to the real world, but for now, with her spread out, nearly incapacitated, he'd make love to her where she lay.

"Do you have the strength to lift your legs for me, my love?

Kenzie raised her thighs without hesitation. She grabbed the head of his cock and guided the tip toward her soaked entrance. They'd need new sheets—no doubt.

The veins in his dick pulsed the instant her skin touched his. His tip slid past her first ring of muscle. As wet as he'd made her, her walls still gripped him tight.

She took him ring by ring, her body thrusting upward in need of more.

Colby watched his cock slide in until he rested inside of her to the hilt. His balls brushed against her cheeks. Maybe one day she'd let him take a picture of himself buried inside of her.

He needed to see it again, as he pulled all the way out to ease back in inch by inch until seated deep. He repeated the move over and over while his thumb rubbed her clit until she orgasmed around his twitching member.

He didn't wait for her second orgasm to abate. He leaned his body closer to hover above her as he slammed deep, forcing another wave of quivers from her channel.

Kenzie reached behind her on instinct for a headboard they didn't have yet. A situation he'd soon rectify.

The wet slap of skin echoed across the walls of the very empty room as she thrust her body in rhythm with his.

Colby quickened his pace. Their moans sang in harmony. "Kenzie, baby, I can't hold out much longer."

"Coat my insides," she screamed.

"Until I'm dripping from you," he screamed back. His body slowed with the last methodic motions of surrender. Trembling, he fell beside her.

He draped his arm across her body. "The very second I can think straight, I'm going to roll you over and go again. When I'm through with you, you won't be able to walk without trembling."

Chapter 49

Kenzie

Kenzie napped with the weight of Colby's arm across her breasts for barely an hour.

She eased her way out from under him, too blissfully happy to sleep anymore.

After she had a cup of coffee in hand, she settled into the wooden swing on the porch of her new home overlooking the mountains to watch the sunrise.

While waiting, she placed a Walmart delivery order for several sets of new sheets. Thankfully, the previous owners had included the washer and dryer in the sale.

Colby joined her as the sun crested the mountains.

His whiskers tickled her lips this morning. She cupped his cheeks and pulled him closer for a deeper kiss while he settled in next to her.

She breathed in deeper. "You smell like me," she said as she inhaled.

"It's the most delicious smell ever created."

Kenzie nestled her head on his shoulder.

"I called in sick today, but I won't be able to tomorrow," Colby told her.

"I guess we better make the most of it, then."

They silently swayed in the calm of the early morning hours.

"I've been thinking," she broached the subject.

"What's that?"

"I think you should go get Cowboy this weekend and bring him home." She bit her lip, worried he might feel pressured.

Colby kissed her forehead. "There's nothing you could say that would make me feel pressured. I'm here to stay. I'm going to set up a meeting with my boss and let him know this is my last job with the company.

"You could come with me this weekend. Help me pack up my condo. I don't have much. The furniture came with the place and stays with it."

"Depends on Leigh. Is she sticking around or leaving?"

Pounding on the front door caught their attention. Colby stood up and peered around the corner of the porch to see who needed them so early.

"Bryce?" he called out.

Bryce took the path leading up to the porch. He pushed his sleeve up and shoved his forearm at Kenzie, revealing a circle matching the position of Leigh's. "Does this have something to do with you?"

Colby's face turned white, remembering the threats Jamie promised. Threats against one of his closest friends.

"I'll kill your sister. Don't think I won't if she hurts him."

"Don't worry. I'll dig the grave."

"What do we tell him?"

"Bryce, sit down." Kenzie motioned to the rocker, also left behind by the homeowners.

Kenzie lifted her sleeve and elbowed Colby to do the same. "Mine and Colby's match. It identifies us as soulmates."

Bryce stared at his on the opposite arm of theirs. He looked up at both of them. A mischievous grin coated his baby face. "Is your sister sporting the one that matches mine?"

"Um, yes," Kenzie admitted.

"I knew I felt something. Something I never felt for anyone before."

"Really, for Leigh?" Colby asked, perplexed. Kenzie elbowed him again.

"When did you get yours?" he asked Colby.

"Probably the same time you did."

Kenzie got comfortable on the swing and gave Bryce the family history leading up to the breaking of the curse and the appearance of the circles.

Bryce let out a long whistle and rubbed his hand through his fine hair.

"I asked her out, you know. She told me,

'Hell no.'"

"There's more," Colby told him.

Kenzie continued the story by letting him know about Jamie's threats.

The mischievous grin appeared on his face again. "Your sister will have to protect me. She won't be able to tell me where to go when I march back to the bar, show her my arm, and ask her out again."

Colby laughed.

Kenzie worried. Worried for her new friend and for Colby. He wouldn't handle anything happening to Bryce.

"I don't know if it's that simple," Kenzie cautioned.

"Simple or not—it's destiny. In no time, she'll fall in love with my charms."

Charms? What charms? This conversation had been the most noise she'd ever heard come out of Bryce's mouth. He rarely spoke whenever she'd been around him. Other than the help he gave her with hacking into police records, he'd said nothing else to her.

Things were going to get interesting for her sister and for Bryce. Kenzie left out the telepathic connection. She figured she'd leave something for him to learn from his soulmate.

Chapter 50

Colby

Colby approached his boss at the end of the day to give him the news.

His boss offered him a raise to entice him to change his mind.

Instantly, his mind pictured Kenzie's belly rounded with their child. A family of his own meant more to him than any number of Benjamins. A part of him hoped his child already grew within her, as they hadn't bothered to use protection. He assumed she wasn't on the pill either because she hadn't planned on ever having sex again.

He probably should bring the subject up sooner rather than later.

At thirty-eight, he wanted a family as soon as possible. His parents had him late, and they had been mistaken many times for grandparents instead of his mother and father.

He hated being an only child and hoped Kenzie had no objections to at least two children.

Thinking of children brought Kenzie's

perfect breasts to the front of his mind, as he rode in the back of the company truck to the Airbnb from the job site.

He didn't get his hands on them until the third time they made love. He greedily sucked at each one before flipping her onto her hands and knees so his hands could hold them while his cock pounded into her sweet pussy.

He might be twelve years her senior, but her need for him would keep him young.

Back at the Airbnb, he packed up everything he owned to carry to the bar. She'd given him a key to *their* place before kissing him goodbye that morning.

He offered to pay for half the house, which she laughed about. She agreed to a compromise. He could pay for the furniture, as long as he didn't have to put any of it on a credit card. She argued there was no reason to start their relationship by going into debt, not when she had more money than she'd ever use.

Colby had enough saved for a down payment on a house for the day he settled down. The day that had finally arrived. He imagined it would cover what they needed to make their house a home. He'd probably have nothing left in his savings, but she again balked that it wouldn't matter.

She told him he'd have to get used to being a kept man.

The picture of her swollen belly came back

to mind. Maybe he could get used to the idea of being a stay-at-home dad. Or maybe he could get his liquor license and convince her to rotate with him at the bar.

He knew she'd never leave the place entirely.

Chapter 51

Kenzie

Kenzie let Leigh update her on Angelina's situation. It turned out, Angelina lost her son when he was born high.

Her sister Ana agreed to take temporary custody. Having grown attached to him, she refused to return him when the court deemed Angelina fit to regain custody.

Ana disappeared with him.

Since Leigh knew where her sister was from the locator spell they'd done on both the sisters, she gave the information to the police who were able to arrest Ana and reunite Angelina with her son.

She waited for her sister to finish before mentioning, "Your soulmate knocked on my door yesterday."

"I know. He showed up here with that goofy grin on his face."

"What are you going to do?"

"I'll keep him safe until we know he's out of danger, but that's it," she bitterly told her sister.

If only Leigh would open up to her, maybe she could help.

Kenzie doubted keeping him safe was how their story would end. Not after experiencing her own pull with destiny.

"I decided to speak on Mom's behalf with the parole board," Leigh changed the subject.

"Oh."

"You should too." It was the softest tone Leigh had used since her unexpected arrival.

Kenzie still hadn't made her mind up. She lived through the worst of their mom's alcohol abuse. Leigh hadn't experienced their mom hitting rock bottom.

"Maybe you should pay her a visit and ask her to tell you about her past. Why she turned to alcohol."

"Because she'll be as forthcoming with me as you have been."

"Leigh and Bryce. Do you realize the jokes we'll be the brunt of just because of our names?"

Leigh walked away. Clearly not wanting to talk anymore.

Remy meandered over with a notebook full of notes. "I've got the whole party planned. Do you have a date in mind yet?"

She rolled her eyes. "I don't even have furniture yet."

"You're going to Georgia this weekend, right? Right." He didn't wait for her answer. "I'll set the date for a month from today. If you don't have furniture, we'll have a dance party like in high school. No one sat down, except to make out."

Kenzie knew better than to argue with him, and he knew her well enough to know if he didn't set a date, she'd go six months without thinking about furnishing her home.

Colby's arms slid around her from behind. His lips grazed the side of her ear. Shivers shot up and down her blood vessels. *Great. How am I going to concentrate tonight?*

"The same way I managed to all day at work."

"Not helping."

"Would it help if I suggested we turn the housewarming party into a wedding as well?"

Her body stiffened. *Is he proposing?*

Colby turned her around to face him. His fingers stroked her cheek, while the other hand slid around her waist and pulled her tight against his chest.

"I guess I am."

She gulped.

"Kenzie Wardwell, marry me."

Lost for words, her head bobbed up and down.

"Crap, now I'm going to have to go to that parole hearing."

"Why?"

"As angry as I am, I can't get married without my mom."

Kenzie's leg jumped up and down as Colby squeezed her hand. The words needed to help her mother hadn't come to her.

Leigh sat on the other side of her. Surprisingly, she allowed Bryce to tag along after Colby told him about it. Both sat close to each other with arms crossed.

As the guards escorted Julie Wardwell into the hearing room, the first thing about her mother that caught her eye was the perfect circle inside of her mother's handcuffed wrist.

How? Her mother didn't deserve a happily ever after. Not after everything she'd done.

Kenzie tuned out the proceedings, her bitterness getting the better of her. Colby gave her hand another gentle squeeze.

A James Bond doppelgänger stood before the parole panel. He raised his arms with the sheet of paper clutched in his palms to read the letter he'd written. Kenzie didn't know who the man was, but the circle sticking from under his wristwatch caught her eye. Her curiosity made her pay close attention to what he had to say.

He cleared his throat before beginning.

"Dear Parole Board,

My name is Tyler Baldwin. Five years ago today, Ms. Julie Wardwell took everything from me. My daughter Kathy was only twenty-three. Her husband Mark, twenty-five. My grandson, Beau, was eighteen months old and my granddaughter, Jodi, had just turned three. It's taken me all this time, but I stand before you today to tell you that I forgive her. It's my understanding that if she is granted parole that she will be ordered to spend the rest of her sentence in community service. My daughter and son-in-law had bought a cabin that they planned to turn into a bed-and-breakfast. It was their dream for their family, and it sits abandoned. I'm asking the court to consider granting her probation that she might help me make my family—the family she stole's—dream a reality. Thank you for your time."

His letter sucked all the air out of every set of lungs in the room. Not only had he offered their mother forgiveness, he wanted her to work for him.

Tyler's ability to forgive her mother gave Kenzie the words she'd desperately tried to form over the last several days.

She hadn't bothered to catch her mother's eyes until walking to the stand in front of the parole board. The smile her mother offered her didn't reach her eyes. Nor did the one Kenzie returned.

"I didn't know what I was going to say today. After listening to Mr. Baldwin forgive my mother, maybe I can work on that, too. Not today, but maybe in the future. If Mr. Baldwin is sincere in his petition for my mother's help to make his family's dream come true, I think the court should grant the petition—for his sake—not so much for hers."

Kenzie's legs trembled on her way back to her seat. Leigh grabbed her hand in reassurance as she approached for her turn. The first bit of affection her sister offered came when she needed it most, as her sister pushed all the comfort of her touch into her spirit.

Chapter 52

Colby

Colby watched the mother-daughter reunion from the booth he sat in with Bryce.

Kenzie asked for privacy, but it didn't stop him from tuning in. A perk he quickly figured out how to do after Kenzie explained to him all about *the soulmate call.*

Julie Wardwell looked very much like the two women she gave birth to. The crow's feet decorating her eyes spoke volumes about the hardships she'd endured.

His fiancée wouldn't find forgiveness for her mother overnight, and he didn't blame her.

Leigh had picked her up from the prison, while Kenzie used the excuse that being shorthanded since losing Jamie made it impossible for her to go.

They all knew her excuse had more to do with not wanting to go than the issue of employee shortage, but nobody pointed it out.

"Welcome home, Mom," Kenzie awkwardly told her mother with the bar separating them.

"Hi, baby." Her mom's endearment triggered a tear.

Kenzie'd built a thick wall around her heart, but her love for her mother still ran deep. He felt it.

She'd told him she needed to do this alone, but it didn't last long when she looked over at him and beckoned him to join them.

At fifty-five, Julie was old enough to be his mother. Something he thanked his lucky stars for. He was not sure what Kenzie would have thought had her mother been closer to his age than she was.

Colby took a seat. Not his regular seat, and he noticed the difference in the imprint on the cushion.

"Mom, this is Colby Parrish. My fiancé. We're getting married in a few weeks and we'd like you to be there."

Colby had seen the circle on her mom's wrist and on Tyler's. Kenzie and he hadn't spoken about what either of them saw or what it meant. Surely, Julie at least knew the Wardwell doom no longer hung over any of their heads.

Not wanting to be left out, Bryce hopped onto the stool next to Colby. "I'm Leigh's soulmate."

Leigh scoffed. "Keep dreaming."

"It's nice to meet you both." Julie offered her hand to them.

It would take time for the three of them to get back to a sense of normalcy.

"Come on, Mom, I'll show you the room upstairs Kenzie converted into an apartment."

Julie turned and grabbed Kenzie's hand. "It might not mean anything to you, but I cast a spell over myself after the accident. Alcohol, to me, is literally poisonous."

Kenzie pulled her hand away and nodded at her mother before walking away to take someone's order.

Colby laughed, watching Bryce's eyes follow Leigh like a lovesick puppy dog.

Leigh and Kenzie combined their magic to put Bryce and Colby under a protective spell. The Somes wouldn't be able to do anything to the two of them magically *if* they did get their powers back. As humans, they were actually more dangerous. They would never see poison in their beer, a gun, or a bus coming.

They'd all have to remain vigilant.

A part of them hoped Jamie's threats were just an empty bluff, but they weren't taking any chances.

Chapter 53

Colby

Much to Remy's disappointment, the living room furniture wouldn't be delivered for another month.

Kenzie and Colby agreed an empty living room made for a better wedding arrangement with chairs lined up like in a chapel.

Instead of wedding invitations, they posted a flyer at the bar. Everyone they wanted at the wedding would see it, including his co-workers.

He personally invited his parents and cousins over the phone.

Remy designated himself giver-away-of-the-bride before she asked him.

Colby stood in his tux, microphone in hand, waiting for Remy and Kenzie to step through the front door.

Bryce pressed play on the karaoke machine they'd carried over to use for the night as soon as the hinges creaked.

Colby swallowed back tears threatening to take control when the sight of Kenzie in her white dress hit him hard. He needed his voice to sing his vows while Kenzie walked toward him.

The melody played as she drew closer. Her arm resting in the crook of Remy's arm. His voice cracked as the words he vowed to his bride escaped his lips.

"Forever can never be long enough for me
Feel like I've had long enough with you
Forget the world now we won't let them see
But there's one thing left to do
Now that the weight has lifted
Love has surely shifted my way
Marry me
Today and every day
Marry me"

Remy placed her hand in his while he continued to sing "Marry Me" by Train. Neither wanted traditional vows nor felt the need to write their own when there were so many songs with the words already written to describe their love for one another.

Colby handed the microphone to Kenzie when his song finished.

Bryce didn't delay starting the song she chose for her vows. Neither had told the other ahead of time what they had chosen.

Colby smiled, recognizing Ellie Goudling's "How Long Will I Love You." He'd almost chosen the same song himself.

> "How long will I love you
> As long as stars are above you
> And longer if I can
> How long will I need you
> As long as the seasons need to
> Follow their plan
> How long will I be with you
> As long as the sea is bound to
> Wash up on the sand"

Bryce hurried to join them after stopping the music. He'd gone online and gotten certified to officiate for them.

Singing their own vows left Bryce with very little to do.

"Colby Parrish, do you take Kenzie Wardwell to be your lawfully wedded wife?"

"I do."

"Kenzie Wardwell, do you take Colby Parrish to be your lawfully wedded husband?"

"I do."

Leigh walked over and handed Bryce the rings.

Kenzie didn't want a diamond ring. She felt it would put her in danger wearing a flashy diamond at the bar. She was happy with the band he placed on her finger.

"With this ring I thee wed."

Kenzie placed his ring on his finger and repeated the words. "With this ring I thee wed."

"By the powers of the internet, I pronounce you man and wife," Bryce proudly shouted over the clapping room full of people who loved both of them.

Colby pulled Kenzie toward him. The need to kiss his bride couldn't wait another second.

"I got you a wedding present," she whispered while their lips collided as husband and wife.

"We said no presents."

"You tell that to your son or daughter. I don't think I can return them."

Realization dawned in Colby's heart. He pulled away from her and held her at a distance. His hand cupped her abdomen.

He looked back up at her, unspeakable joy poured from every crevice of her face.

Colby scooped her from behind and spun her around the room.

Bryce introduced to the room: Mr. and Mrs. Colby Parrish.

Bonus Chapter

Abigail Somes Jr.

1720

Mother's obsession with my pitiful excuse of a father makes her weak. The proof of what Abigail already knew came to her when she received the sight she thought she'd inherit from her grandmother.

Walking through the woods near the home mother and she built after her father's death, her first vision came upon her without warning, like a rattlesnake's bite. The poisonous strike hits his victims before they even see his body slithering through the grass.

She despised the Turner blood coursing through her veins. A gift from the man who'd fertilized her mother's egg.

No love resided in Abigail's heart for Jeremiah Turner. The man who made her mother weak. Men were a means to an end. Use them to reproduce and toss them aside. They weren't capable of love.

How many women came to her and her mother because their husbands beat them or didn't come home at night because they spent the night burying their prick in some whore?

The Somes women survived off the pain men caused women. They'd come up with the perfect revenge for their clientele.

One drop of their potion, and their husband's prick never stood erect again.

Her first vision showed her the doom her family would face because of their enemies, the Wardwell sisters.

Not only would a Wardwell strip the Somes of their powers, but a Wardwell's coupling with a Turner would mean the end of their powers.

Abigail's screams shook the trees. What she'd seen in the future terrified her to her bones.

Her only consolation—it wouldn't happen in her lifetime. Yet she couldn't stand by and do nothing.

"Father of shadows, be my witness. The Wardwell women will never find love with a man. Like the piss poor women who show up on my doorstep, so will my enemies know the same sorrows."

Abigail searched for a clearing. She lay prostrate upon the spot she deemed perfect. Lightning probably struck the area void of life, while the trees, flowers, and grass thrived all around it.

Determined to remain with her face to the ground until a solution presented itself, she prayed to her benefactor. Begging for the perfect snare.

Her great, great, great granddaughter would need an advantage. She'd need a way to find the wretched Turner before her enemy.

After days without food or water, lying with her face in the dirt, her finger moved in a circle. As if something took control of her digit, it drew the symbol repeatedly. She couldn't stop herself. Not even when blood seeped from the pad of her finger.

Only once realization dawned on her did her finger stop.

"Mark my enemies and theirs." She commanded of the circle filled with the combined blood of a Turner and a Somes. As soon as her command left her lips, she blew upon the dirt.

The wind carried her spell and her will until finding her enemies and theirs. Marking each one of them unknowingly with her symbol. To be seen only by those with her blood.

A wicked smirk curved the edges of her mouth.

"My children have a chance. The gift I give my daughters will enable them to defeat our enemies once and for all."

Abigail raised her head in mockery. A chilling cackle filled the night sky. The birds sleeping in the trees took flight for fear of what had disturbed their slumber.

She rose from the dirt, confident that a Wardwell would never take away her family's power.

***Keep flipping for an unedited sample from Leigh and Bryce's story. Coming August 2023.**

Author's Note

If you haven't read the first installment of *The Soulmate Call* and you enjoyed this story, I hope you grab a copy and immerse yourself in Rey's and Lisabeth's story.
While this series is best read in the order written, it is not crucial.

If you read this story, a review on Amazon or Goodreads is so appreciated. Good or bad.

Find all my social media links and book links on https://linktr.ee/tiffanyannbooks

The Wardwell Witches: Coming 2023

The Witch's Journey – Leigh & Brice

The Witch's Redemption – Julie & Tyler

Previous Titles

The Soulmate Call- Rey's & Lisabeth's story

The Soulmate Battle – Caleb's & Pasiphae's story

The Soulmate Restoration- Luke's & Danielle's story

The Soulmate Healing – Cole's & Darion's story

The Soulmate Rekindled – Scott's & Kelly's story

The Soulmate Triangle – Caleb's & Avery's story

The Soulmate Dilemma – Samuel's & Samantha's story

The Soulmate Homecoming – Benjamin's & Sarah's story

The Soulmate Beginning – Ezekiel's & Annabelle's story

The Soulmate Reunion – Meg's & Jack's story

The Soulmate Circle – Aeson's & Mercy's story

Hotel Lamia Series

Hotel Lamia: Where Immortals Sleep

Hotel Lamia New York

Hotel Lamia Casablanca

Hotel Lamia: Return to New Orleans

The Witch's Journey

Chapter 1

Leigh

Destiny found me at age fourteen, turning me into the killer that I am. My sister has no idea. I don't want her to ever see who I've become.

Even though deep down, I know she'd understand. Since returning home, my conscience nags at me, reminding me that Kenzie would have done the same things I've done for humanity if the roles were reversed.

I tell myself I'm protecting her, but somewhere in the recesses of my mind, I know I resent her.

Why me? I'm the youngest. Destiny always comes for the oldest. Responsibilities come with the territory when you're born first.

2013

The first day of high school. I finally made it. No more junior high bullies. I've been told that part of my life ended when I became a freshman. High school students are more focused and past that awkward stage between childhood and teenagerhood.

Mama always told me 'That we make plans and God laughs.' I didn't quite get what she meant until the new transfer student airdropped a photo of Becky Lynn coming out of the girl's bathroom with the back of her skirt tucked into her underwear.

Opening my phone to check why it vibrated in between classes, I didn't even catch of glimpse of the hurtful photo before my witchy senses kicked in. Yep, I call the witchy senses—similar to Spidey senses like Spiderman.

How do I put into words, being shredded from the inside out not just physically, but emotionally when overloaded with the knowledge a Somes witch lurked nearby causing pain and destruction?

It's not just a feeling I get. This one was my first. Mama had explained it to Kenzie and me, but she failed at making me comprehend the depth of it.

Kids videoed me—the freak—spazing in the hallway like I'd just walked into the tornado simulator at the zoo.

I couldn't care less what my peers thought of me as I writhed out of control.

By the time someone grabbed a teacher to check on me, I'd come out of my witchy moment. Sweat poured from by brow into my eyes. I used the sleeve of my shirt to clear my vision.

Mr. Smith encouraged me to head to the nurse's station. I assured him I'd head there, but I had no intention of bothering the school nurse with something she couldn't help me with.

I watched the video sent to me that activated my witchy senses before forwarding it to my mom with a text explaining I'd had my first brush with destiny.

At home, Mama handed me the dagger spelled to kill my first Somes. I'm fourteen, damn it —too young for my first kill.

While the hand carved family heirloom, I held captivated my attention. The attention to detail in the carvings of two W's intertwined amidst a burst of light held my admiration.

Mama explained to me that her mother gave her one when fate warned her of a nearby witch who needed killing.

"One day, you'll spell knives for your daughters as well. All it takes is a plunge to the heart, and to dust she returns."

I shoved the knife back toward Mama. "Can't you do it?" I begged.

She hung her head and shook it from side to

side. "I'd be remiss in taking your responsibility to spare you. This is our destiny. It's why we have our powers. Fate would have called me if I was meant to find her and take her out."

Laying in bed playing the situation over and over in my head, I refused to accept that fate or destiny would demand a fourteen year snuff out another teenager.

I scrolled through the hateful messages, still being sent in response to the video. Messages telling the girl that in order to save herself the embarrassment of returning to school, she should kill herself. The number of teenagers push the same agenda turned my stomach, but not as much as my responsibility to stop the Somes from ever doing something similar to another person again.

A Somes sending this kind of video into the world had to have been laced with a spell prompting the savage volatile behavior toward the girl most had never even met.

The many peptalks I gave myself before the sun rose didn't do the trick. I had no choice. I refused to become a killer at fourteen.

So I ran.

Chapter 2

Bryce

Do you know how many times I laid in bed at night jerking off while watching the Halliwell sisters on my TV.

Don't judge me. I'm a red-blooded, fully functioning male. A shy one at that. My shyness has kept me from losing the one thing every man dreams about losing—my virginity. My one secret I'll take to my grave with me.

My brain didn't believe Colby when he told me the woman who'd turned him to a pile of mush was a witch. A real honest to goodness witch.

I wanted to believe him. My shameful obsession with the sisters from *Charmed* made me wish Colby spoke the truth—for his sake.

As much as I wanted my friend to have a hot witch to come home to every night, it never occurred to me to wish for her to have a sister.

Only she does.

Leigh Wardwell. I didn't know she was Kenzie's sister the first time I laid eyes on her. I only knew that the storm cloud raging behind her grey eyes caught my attention.

The chip on her shoulder coupled with the steel walls surrounding her countenance emboldened me.

It's one thing to wonder if a pretty girl is going to shoot your advances down. It's another thing to know she will beyond a shadow of a doubt.

I had nothing to lose when I approached her. I knew she said no, but I knew she'd have to speak to me when she did.

Having the memory of her voice speaking to me would get me through the long, lonely nights.

Waking up in the night with searing pain in my arm to discover a circle tattoo on my arm that I knew I hadn't put there gave me hope.

I didn't know what it meant, but I knew it had something to do with the lovely witches who'd come into my life.

Once Kenzie explained the circle and my connection to Leigh, I skipped to the bar. I'm certain the grin I wore made me look like an idiot.

I am under no delusions that winning Leigh's heart will come easy. She's cold as ice. I'm prepared to be the man to do what it takes to thaw her heart.

She laughed when I revealed my circle identical to hers. Anyone else would have missed it, but I caught the brief glimpse of hope that flickered in her eyes.

Between my shyness and the walls of Jericho boxing her in—we make quite the pair.

I have little confidence in my abilities to charm a woman, but I have loads of faith in destiny.

Besides, she's stuck with me as long as the threat toward me hangs over us both. I should be scared, but all I feel is gratitude.

Whatever she is running from might slow our inevitable love story, but it won't keep her from making sure some crazy ex-witch family doesn't take me out to punish her.

I'm the kid who patiently sucked on a two-inch jaw breaker without giving into the urge to bite into it before reaching the sweet tart center.

I completely understand why Colby sat at the bar every night just to get a glimpse of Kenzie.

As long as Leigh waited tables, helping out at *The Witch's Brew,* in her section is where I'd be every night.

About the Author

More than twenty years after studying English at the University of New Orleans, Tiffany Ann is excited to be living out her dream of putting her stories on paper and sharing them. Writing contemporary paranormal romances with a splash of science fiction and magical realism. Her books are meant for anyone whose heart believes in true love.

Born and raised outside New Orleans, she is married to her soulmate and is the mother of four teenagers, and is extremely proud of her Louisiana heritage, going back eight generations. Tiffany works in the hotel industry and serves on several boards, benefiting her community. Her favorite movie is "The Princess Bride" and her favorite book is "Wuthering Heights."

Tiffany loves to read and support indie authors living the same dream she is, and loves to hear from fans.